DAMIEN GOES TO HELL

By Bill Jonas

AVERNUS PRESS
LONG BEACH, CALIFORNIA

DAMIEN GOES TO HELL

Copyright © 2011 Bill Jonas

The characters and events in this book are fictitious. Any similarity to real
persons, living or dead, is coincidental and not intended by the author.

Published by Avernus Press
Long Beach, CA 90803

ISBN 978-061554804-3

Book design, photos and cover illustration by Bill Jonas

Damien Goes to Hell

Contents

Foreword

The following text was developed from an outline I had devised for a rock opera project. The project required a storyline as a basis for the lyrics, then the outline of the story was used to develop the props and sets for the live show.

The backstory of the book, then, is that a young rock band is seeking inspiration to create a unique stage show. They decide to spend a night in a local haunted house with the hope of igniting the creative spark that would make the project spectacular.

While in the house, they discover a hidden panel that leads to a small study lined with old books and a large wooden writing table. Upon closer inspection, the leather chair in front of the desk still holds the skeletal remains of the owner. On the table, next to the dusty Underwood typewriter is a neat pile of double-spaced typewritten pages, the unpublished manuscript for a book entitled "Damien Goes to Hell", c. 1901.

The band members take turns reading from the manuscript by candlelight in the small library in the company of the skeleton of the author, who is now sporting a beer in one hand and a cigarette in the other. They realize before long that the story would make an inspired basis for their rock show and begin making plans to build sets and props...

Chapter 1

A Bad Day in Ambrosia

Damien looked out over the anxious crowd from atop the makeshift scaffold in the town square. The raw heat of their collective wrath burned away his invisibility, laying bare his weakened soul to their humiliation. Snatched from the shadows of breadlines and day labor, he had previously eluded the judgemental spotlight of the properly socialized, more often reduced to nothingness owing to their indifference to his very existence. But on that day, he was the center of their attention.

"He's *killed* her! Murderer!" The words tormented his desperate mind — the love of his life snuffed out and he alone to bear the blame.

The next day, the *Vedette Messenger* featured a grand spread in the Society section on the life and death of poor Miss Rachel Hart, with scarcely a mention of how the angry mob had chased him down the street.

* * *

As a lad, Damien would cringe when he heard that creaky wooden door slam, his father dumping his street-sweeping implements in a heap. "*Boy!*" That gin-soaked syllable would resonate through the empty flat. "I *told* youse to stay away from them *fancy* girls. They'se parents wanna take my job away now!" And the belt would come off.

As bad as the whippings hurt, Damien knew it was the booze, the poverty and the perpetual frustration of his dismal social status that ate at his old man. Earlier, Damien had been in the park on the other side of the tracks from his neighborhood. The park was the nearest place he knew where flowers would grow, and he gathered a bouquet to place at his mother's grave.

Rachel and her playmates lived in grand Victorian mansions surrounding the verdant commons set with sculpted topiary and a proper playground for proper young men and women. They had seen the poor boy in the park near the playground before and even spoken to him on occasion, though it was more often a snide comment whispered through a brocade sunbonnet, followed by cruel laughter. Except for Rachel. Whether she felt pity or thought she saw worthwhile qualities in him that the others had missed eluded even her. She missed every opportunity to poke fun at him and even spoke kindly to him when he would approach.

This day was no exception. It was the cruel laughter wafting through the summer humidity that stole away his smile and the gentle voice of Rachel that brought it back.

When the gaggle of nannies appointed to watch over the girls noticed young Damien in their midst, they issued stern warnings, causing the girls to withdraw. Only Rachel remained.

"Who are the flowers for?" she asked.

"Th-they are for you," Damien stammered, handing her the bouquet.

Then it was Rachel's turn for a reprimand. Her nanny plucked the bunch of flowers from her hand and flung them to the ground to punctuate her scolding. Still, as she was being led away from the park, Rachel shared a shy, lip-biting smile with Damien.

* * *

Damien saw Rachel around town on occasion through the ensuing years, usually as he was sweeping up after some gala social function, and she was being courted and wooed by some "worthy" suitor. In the end, she was to be seen at the elbow of the despicable Rupert Wickersham, whose family owned a majority of the town. Rachel's family owned much of what was left, so a future marriage arranged to bring the two families together seemed inevitable to the socialites.

Wickersham, though twice her age, found himself attracted to Rachel long before she became an eligible debutant. He remembered fondly the warm afternoons, sitting on the bench in the playground with a newspaper spread across his lap, his hand shoved deep in his pocket, studying the young girls playing hopscotch. The golden tresses beckoning, the wispy blue play dress rising and falling with every skip in the fragrant summer breeze... rising and falling... the monogrammed silk kerchief dabbing moisture from his perspiring brow.

And now she would be his trophy, one for which he had long waited, despite that he was a man not obliged to wait for things that he wanted. Yet it bore no end of misery for Wickersham to know that he was utterly unable to possess even the smallest cockle of Rachel's heart. She spoke to him as a servant would speak to a humorless master: Eyes averted, emotionless and without candid conversation. Her life had been mapped out since before she charted her first hopscotch board on the sidewalk. She had only to walk through her part and recite her lines and hers would be the consummate life, such was the hard-boiled advice of her parents. Yet it severely tested her assiduously learned social graces to appear content as the future Missus Wickersham.

Damien hated the sadness in her eyes. At every opportunity, the pair escaped together for a brief interlude to fantasize of an alternate life, free of all the social constraints that caused them each such tribulation and pain. As often happened, at the height of their reverie, innocent eyes would meet and a forbidden kiss would be shared, which would never fail to bring reality crashing down upon them both, causing them each to resign to their own respective world.

* * *

The town of Ambrosia was considered a respectable town by most accounts. The cobblestone streets were kept in good repair and the watering troughs by the hitching posts were always full; the mayor kissed babies and the church bells rang on Sunday morning. When the railroad went through, it lent the town the means to grow, but it also brought with it disparate points of view.

Bitter acrimony arose when the town council approved the application of a local theatrical-arts group to present an All-Hallowed Saints program on the court-house lawn. The shows were considered heresy, even blasphemy, by the church — banned for all the appearances of glorifying the power of Lucifer. The theatrical supporters argued that it was the group's endeavor to illustrate the horrors of evil, and that the program was devised as a celebration to exorcise the evil spirits from the town. For their part, the townsfolk believed that it might be fun to don gruesome costumes for one night of the year and partake of the local hard cider tasting, so the church administrators were caused to relent.

* * *

To draw in the younger crowd, the group enlisted a popular local band named Pigasus (for the flying pig drawn on the front of the bass drum). The lads' rowdy attire was attributed more to their participation in the Hallowe'en festivities than to any radical cultural statement, even though what they wore was unexceptional streetwear by their own thinking.

Damien lost himself in the lyric, his vocals rising above the din of the band. He sang out loud in the midst of the sleepy little town, never making contact with the eyes that had looked down on him all those years. Invisible revelers milled about before the scaffold until he was surprised to recognize a kindred sprit among them.

"Rachel, is that you?"

Damien signaled his bandmates to downshift to one of their melodic original songs, which happened to take the form of a paean to a lost love. Her eyes welled a bit when she realized that the song was written for her, penned by one who had become quite dear.

As the band returned to popular standards, Rachel's own lilting voice joined in duet with Damien's. For the moment, the pair soared above the crowd. Then, after the set ended, it was Rachel's hand wiping the sweat from Damien's brow, around the corner of the courthouse, out of sight from the crowd. But it was Wickersham's cruel eyes that witnessed the warm embrace and saw the smiling eyes of his future bride for the first time. The thorny shrubbery trembled from the nervous voyeur hiding within; narrowed yellowy eyes watched Damien ascend the steps to the stage. Wickersham rushed from his cover to confront Rachel.

Damien was beaming and his performance was stellar, though short-lived.

Wickersham's voice interrupted the final chorus, "Come see ... see what he's done! He's killed her ... my dear Rachel is dead!" His quivering accusatory digit pointing out Damien as the culprit; the slumped body dressed in white just visible behind the shrubbery.

"No!" cried Damien. "This can't be ... he is lying!"

Then Wickersham lifted the limp body, displaying her to the townsfolk. The audience became a murmuring crowd; the crowd became a seething mob. Damien bounded from the back of the scaffold and into the door of the courthouse. He would have to defend his innocence at another time.

The courthouse clerks looked up from their paperwork to see the blur of a young man in desperation running in one door and out the other, followed at a short interval by an angry mob with vengeance in mind.

Damien sprang from the door on the opposite side of the courthouse, running down the block to a familiar alley where he often found sanctuary as a boy. He dragged the heavy iron cover aside and disappeared into a yawning manhole, down the ladder into the darkness...

Chapter 2

The Stolen Light

A disturbing presence lurked in the darkness. Narrowed yellowy eyes peered out over the embroidered silken quilt and seeing naught, disappeared back under the covers.

"Wickersham."

There it was again. A raspy whisper in the darkness.

Or was it? A twig rubbing against the window, perhaps. Or the faint echoes of animal lust issuing from the servants' quarters in the basement.

"Wickersham!"

Bony fingers withdrew the covers, trembling the entire quilt.

"I SAW YOU!"

A burst of fiery light... a thunderclap rattled the room. Billowing toxic sulfur smoke burned his eyes. Paralyzed by the sight of The Beast manifest, Wickersham could not look away.

"You strangled a virtuous young lady, one who was to be your wife."

"It wasn't me! I — I didn't..." Wickersham whimpered.

You are a MURDERER!" bellowed Lucifer to his face, "AND you are a coward and a liar! And as such, your soul is mine for this life and beyond."

The Beast paced with heavy, deliberate steps, floor-boards creaking, the room shaking with each footfall.

"Please don't kill me," Wickersham begged.

"I am not here to kill you," Lucifer said. "Hell abounds with fools like you. The soul of a virtuous maiden is worth legions of your type. I want the girl!"

Wickersham realized that Rachel would be buried in her family plot, which was on hallowed ground in the cemetery next to the church. Lucifer's operatives would be unable to retrieve her soul from there.

"What can I do?" Wickersham pleaded. "Anything!"

"Have her buried in your family graveyard," Lucifer scoffed. "Certainly no saved souls were ever planted there!"

"What if I can't convince them? Th-they all hate me."

"Then my minions will come for YOU!" Lucifer snorted. And with that, the apparition disappeared, leaving only the empty darkness.

Despite the lust he had felt for his young fiancée, and the fact that it was by his own hand that she was removed not only from the daylight of the living world, but also removed from the very Eternal Light to which all souls strive, any tears that streaked the fine satin pillow were owed but to the burn of the brimstone smoke in his eyes.

* * *

The entire town turned out for Rachel's wake, for she was held in high regard and liked by all.

The graveside mass, by contrast, attracted a very small contingency of her cohorts. Most gave the excuse that they weren't up to traveling out of town, though more likely, they had succumbed to the legends of the Wickersham graveyard being a place possessed by dark forces. Numerous sightings of incorporeal manifestations had been made there, reported by more than one terrified wayfarer. Although, the testimony was always withdrawn as quick as a trespassing citation could be introduced.

Rachel's father had been against allowing her to be buried in the Wickersham plot. He had purchased a plot for her among his ancestral family, and was bound to see her in it. But there had been a deal struck some time ago, wherein he would receive an equal partnership in a prospering oilfield that the Wickershams controlled, in exchange for his daughter's hand in marriage. That offer increased suddenly to full ownership in exchange for the burial rights, and the offer was accepted in a most expedient manner.

The attendant preacher, better known to most as the town lush, could most often be found sleeping on a park bench. And, although having been forcefully removed from the church for his drunken outbursts, was occasionally called upon to perform last rights for wayward folk and drifters not deemed worthy of a proper burial, and was the only one who would report to the Wickersham graveyard in any case. He arrived late and short of breath from the long walk spoke over the open coffin to the small gathering, .

"Dearly beloved, we have gathered here today to mourn the loss of our invaluable loved one. In the sweat of thy face shalt thou eat bread 'til thou returnest unto the ground from whence thou wast taken. Ashes to ashes, dust to dust. God rest ye weary bones. Amen."

"Amen."

And just as quickly, he was off. Cradling a wooden crate of single-malt scotch retrieved from behind a crumbling mausoleum, he had set a brisk pace in the direction of town, wanting to put every possible footstep between himself and that loathsome boneyard before sundown. The flock of mourners were not far behind.

A solitary figure moved among the decrepit headstones. Damien crept in silence to within sight of Rachel's grave. There he waited to see if others were coming before he could say his final farewells.

He would be unable to secure the services of any attorneys in the village, he believed. They were all either retained by Wickersham, or would charge a ridiculous fee to go up against him. The town constabulary wouldn't be of any help either — in fact, they were probably tracking him already at the behest of both Wickersham and Rachel's parents.

No, his only option would be to go far away and start over. Before he could go, however, one last goodbye was in order.

As Damien emerged from behind a faded, mossy headstone, a rustling in the underbrush caused him to retreat in fear. He caught but a glimpse of a creature like none he had seen before: wicked eyes and a stout muzzle that snarled as it sniffed the air, searching. He recalled a dire wolf from a book he saw as a child, though he knew them to be extinct. Convinced he was about to be eaten, he tried to wrestle a block of limestone from a nearby monument for defense.

And then there were two of them, growling and hissing with jaws snapping, savoring the final moment before closing in on their quarry. As Damien tried to back away in stealth, a twig snapped and he was found out. Two pairs of fiery, nefarious eyes glared at him from the darkening labyrinth of tombstones. His heavy heart sank as he realized he was probably not capable of effective fight or flight under the circumstances. He took solace in the idea that he might soon be rejoined with his beloved.

The glowing red eyes regarded Damien for a moment and then were distracted, searching for something else. They had not come for the living. They were scavengers, seeking only the newly dead, those with a living soul still tethered, however tenuous. When they discovered Rachel's coffin, they pawed the ground, snorting in triumph. Their piercing howls reverberated between the timeworn limestone markers, calling out in the twilight. It wasn't long before they were answered.

It seemed that the air itself was transformed over the surreal scene, becoming at once close and dreadful. As the howling subsided, the night fell silent. The gloomy chorus of katydids, amphibians and nightwings was muted in the dense fog by the approach of a disquieting presence.

In an instant, the thick silence was torn asunder by a monstrous roar and vicious snarling growls. The hellhounds had located their prey, now Asmodeus, the powerful archduke of Lucifer's army came to claim the body. Damien could but watch, mortified, as the great hairy beast retrieved the corpse of his dear friend, carried off then as a rag doll into the dark woods, flanked by the vicious scavengers.

Damien's consciousness escaped him under the ponderous weight of the situation. He regained it as a black owl appeared on a branch just above him, startling him with its resounding call. A moment before, the hoot of the owl had been the distant call of a lover, pleading to be rescued in some mysterious dream; awakened, it became a call to action in the living nightmare that had just unfolded before him.

Running his hand along the rail of the empty casket, Damien noticed the bouquet of white roses that Rachel had been given to hold in her eternal sleep. He picked them up and breathed in the sweet scent of rose petals caressed by the jasmine perfume that Rachel had favored. What could he do to help her now? He wouldn't be able to enlist any assistance from the townsfolk. They would more likely lynch him before he was halfway through his incredulous tale.

As his horror began to recede, he was overpowered by a desperate loneliness... alone in the dark graveyard with no road leading to any home. Only the song remained. The one he had meant for her to hear. The one then pouring from his wounded heart and sounding from his trembling lips.

A light snow began to fall, caressing the empty casket.

* * *

There is a region between life and death, a place where the soul, still cooling from its deceased body, is reoriented to the spiritual realm. Just as leaving that realm — being born into the physical world — is a confusing blur, reentering the spirit world leaves one reeling and dazed. During this period, a soul is vulnerable to the dark forces that would entice the naïve newcomers away from the Light and into corruption.

In this region there exist souls that are temporarily suspended in their freefall into Hell by virtue of the fact that their sins were of a forgivable nature. Unlike the souls that have ascended to the Light, they have retained their skeletal frames until they can prove themselves worthy to shed their bones, or "gain their wings", as they say. It is their lot in death to assist the newly departed, to keep them from falling victim to the dark forces.

* * *

The ground had been disturbed there — the snow didn't lie over that one grave as it did on the rest of the ground. Damien walked wide around the plot, taking care not to step onto any of the snowless ground. The rising full moon illuminated the incised lettering on the marker: "Pluribus". Except that the carving was worn — not a fresh grave as he had first supposed. Grave robbers, he wondered? The thought caused him to pause for a moment and search the perimeter of the graveyard.

"Asmodeus." The feeble voice of an old man broke the crisp night air, causing Damien to jump.

"Wh-who are you?" Damien found himself confronting the long-dead countenance of a man attired in what was once a fine-tailored butler suit, mostly decomposed and hanging in tatters from his skeletal frame. Though he should have been properly terrified, he regarded the presence as more hideous than threatening.

"I am Pluribus, at your service," said the dead one, touching the brim of his derby. "It was Asmodeus who stole the girl, sir."

Pluribus was propped up against a granite urn several feet from his grave, but there were no footprints. There was no decomposed moonshadow cast next to that of the urn. Damien imagined that he may have yet been asleep, suffering night terrors, but the cold and hunger felt very real.

"Who is Asmo—?"

"Asmodeus is the archduke of Hell," Pluribus said. "He comes for the dead."

"Rachel... is there any way I can get her back?"

"Her soul is in Hell, sir. You would risk all to get in — make no plans for any return."

"I have naught to return for," Damien said, downcast.

"As you say, sir," Pluribus replied, "though it would require dark sorcery to find your path."

"Can you show me the way?" Damien asked .

"No, sir," said Pluribus. "I no longer serve the living. I served two generations of Wickershams and am left in this undead state for my trouble. The Elder raped my daughter; the Younger raped my wife. Although my revenge escaped detection by the living, my transgressions were not hidden from the Spiritual world. Now I must pay my penance by assisting the dead. Once they are in Hell, however, they are beyond my reach."

"What can I do to help Rachel?"

"There is one who knows such secrets, if you dare ask. Follow the mountain road beyond the pass to the old stone fortress. There resides Draconus the conjurer. If you carry a sheaf of witch grass or wolfbane, he may hear you out. But beware — the spirits in the old fortress died uneasy and will not welcome your presence."

"I will do what is required." Damien found himself alone in the graveyard talking to himself. The hooting of an owl in the distance echoed in response.

Chapter 3

In the House of Arkenstone

The wind howled through the mountain pass sending whirlwinds skating down the steep road. A procession of black vultures floated along the thermals that radiated from the rocky face of the mountain. The morning sun painted the crumbling stone fortress crimson against the craggy purple background. A once proud castle, ancient battles had shattered its walls, save for the inner chambers and dungeons carved deep into the mountain.

Damien had never quite believed the stories about the hermit sorcerer living alone in the haunted castle, and said to be more than three hundred years old. It was mentioned in at least one alehouse version of the yarn that Draconus the Conjurer held the key to turn lead into gold. The story contends that the mad king Arkenstone, who lived more than two centuries ago, had summoned Draconus to the old stone fortress, requesting him to fill the north tower with gold bullion. In exchange he would receive the Staff of Merr, which holds great power for those who know how to use it, and great danger for those who do not — and which the conjurer had long coveted. As Draconus proceeded with his alchemy, the king's advisor was busy counseling his majesty on the benefits of the idea that Draconus should be executed upon completion of the task, lest he provide the same service to the other kingdoms, thereby bringing down the worth of gold. The king agreed with his reasoning and signed the order.

However, Draconus learned of this treachery and escaped the castle that night having filled the tower only part way. The door to the tower was left open just enough to allow a shimmering golden cascade to flow out into the public hallway. By morning, most everyone in the castle had claimed a sample of the precious bullion for safe keeping, until the breach was discovered and the door secured. Though by the next day, all who had touched the tainted gold became paralyzed, leaving the bulk of the population lying helplessly about in the court-yards and halls.

By no coincidence then, well-armed battalions of two neighboring kingdoms were marching from opposite ends of the same road to converge at the castle, to lay siege and vanquish the evil king once and for all time. A prolonged bombardment left the battle-scarred walls and towers in rubble; the ensuing carnage left the House of Arkenstone broken and thoroughly vanquished. After the armies, the highwaymen, and finally the vultures, had picked the place threadbare, Draconus took up residence there and there he has lived ever since — or so it has been told.

None had been there in recent times to learn if anyone actually did reside there, likely because of the tales suggesting that none who had gone there before had ever returned.

Damien had heard the stories and recalled them all on his way up the mountain road. Stories that were easily dismissed over a pint are more sobering when the broken fortress walls loom out of the fog on the road ahead. The grayness of the morning helped to dampen his apprehension of the coming encounter. That, and the idea that Wickersham would get away with murder — and that he, himself, would get the blame — further stoked his resolve. Tired, cold and hungry, he constructed a meager torch from a branch and some dried moss, knowing it would be dark in the entrails of the fortress.

* * *

The bats had taken up roost in the stairwell, leaving the worn quarry-block steps slippery with guano. The torchlight was intermittent so Damien had to keep adding more dried moss from his overstuffed pockets. The musty air grew heavier with each step down the long spiral into the dank abyss. Thick layers of cobwebs that covered the front of his clothes attested to the fact that none had passed this way in recent times, and he had to pause to brush away their former residents from time to time.

A black marble archway off the stairway was the first entrance he encountered. A narrow hallway led to a foyer lined with alabaster sculptures of celebrated figures from a forgotten past. Damien saw a larger room beyond, a dim glow emanating from within. A quick gasp of wind that extinguished his light brought with it the distinct scent of something long dead. The room beyond glowed brighter, though he could not detect the source of the light. He was aware of something moving in the foyer next to him — one of the statues was breathing! But it was a warm, easy feeling that overtook Damien, reassuring him, as though he felt among family. And then he recognized her...

"Rachel?" Damien was surprised at the sound of his own voice.

Rachel was radiant, smiling and inviting, the music of her laughter set him at ease. The recent memory of her warm embrace pulled him forward willingly. A small voice within told him to resist, but so great was his desire to see his friend alive that he pushed the voice aside, as he often did when it forbade that which he desired. In this matter, though, the small voice was quit insistent and sent a formidable chill up his spine.

For an instant, the familiar smile flickered. For a mere moment, a crack in the façade revealed a glimpse of horror — those dead black eyes peering from that dusty skull, the broken teeth where those smiling lips had beckoned. Damien pulled himself away, backing out of the hallway as though a stiff wind pushed against him, and fell out onto the stone staircase. He caught himself mere inches from the edge of the abyss.

He found his torch was still in his hand, still burning as before. In a panic, he turned to see if anyone — or anything — was following him out of the hallway, but it had vanished. An impenetrable granite wall extending as far as he could see had replaced the black marble arch, hallway and all. He brushed some of the cobwebs off, shaking his head in disbelief. Damien continued his grim descent, deciding that the scene he had just witnessed was trickery that the sorcerer had put in place to deter visitors.

Damien tried his best to steel himself for the next encounter, whatever that might be. Torchlight danced down the steps before him and caused the various lizards and rodents to scamper further down into the darkness. Then he noticed something out of place: the bones of a human arm lay across one step, with the hand bones arranged to point toward the wall. He moved his torch closer to the wall and saw letters scrawled onto one of the stones: Pluribus.

Breathing a sigh of relief, he pressed on the stone. Nothing happened. Pressed again, harder. Still nothing. Then, bracing himself against the steps, pushed with all of his might. Nothing. Breathing hard, he sat down. It occurred to him that an old man would not have devised anything so physical to gain entry to his chamber, so he reached over and knocked on the stone three times.

A thick, grating sound scraped away the silence as a section of the stone wall was pushed aside, revealing a black marble archway — the scene he had just envisioned! A mirage? It was with great trepidation that Damien entered the same narrow hallway, pausing in the foyer surrounded by stone statuary. He forced himself to confront the figure that had become Rachel moments before, but it was made of stone now, the likeness of a queen from the last dynasty of the living.

On the wall hung several proper torches, so Damien availed of one, leaving his own makeshift one in its stead. Exiting the foyer, he turned to look one last time at the statues. All of the faces glared back at him with menacing looks — his own face fixed in various wicked, punishing scowls. Calling him. Taunting him. He turned away and hurried into the next room. "If the powers of Draconus are such that he can make me afraid of my own reflection, I have much to suffer, I fear."

The next room was empty, carved into the living rock of the mountain; the walls, ceiling and floor were all solid stone. Other than the doorway where he had entered, no other openings were apparent, though the far end of the room receded into the darkness, beyond where his torch-light would reach.

As he set out, he was aware of something underfoot.

Where there had been bare rock now felt supple. He moved the torch nearer the floor to have a closer look and recognized the pattern there — it was the faded floral pattern that carpeted his room as a child. Looking around, he noticed that he was standing next to the rustic metal frame of his childhood bed. The dog-eared picture of his mother on the nightstand; the unstuffed teddy bear with no eyes; the perpetual pile of dirty laundry — all as he recalled. But then he noticed that there was no door, not even the one he had just passed through.

"This is not real!" he declared, marching headlong into a wall — then right through it! Only an illusion; he would not be deterred. He then found himself in the small room under the manhole where he would hide as a street urchin; then in the playground where the privileged children would tease him. A moment later he was back in the vacant stone room, facing a granite wall with a doorway in the middle.

Damien peered into the opening and saw a stairway descending into a lower chamber where a mist that hung in the air luminesced with an aqua blue glow. Eerie moaning sounds morphed into the mewl of a mournful pipe organ that reverberated in the depths. He entered the vision, realizing too late that it was a mirror that had drawn his gaze. The mirror shattered. The shards of glass turned into black bats that swooped low, knocking Damien to the ground, before they disappeared into the darkness. Again he sat before the granite wall with no doorway, no way out.

Again he had to fortify his resolve and refuse to let frustration get the best of him. Realizing that he still heard the muffled sound of the pipe organ, he believed that he was quite close to his destination. He began tapping the stones in the wall where the mirror had been, but nothing moved. He knocked on as many stones as he could before his knuckles grew swollen and sore. It occurred to him then, that if he saw the image of the stairway in a *mirror*, then the *real* stairway must be somewhere behind him.

Starting where the mirror was and edging step by step toward where the stairway *should have been*, he tapped the floor with his toe out in front of him. Reaching out a bit farther, there was a void — a dropoff. He eased his foot over the edge until it landed on an unseen step below. The stairs had been there all along, only hidden by illusion. He stepped down into what appeared to be a solid granite floor, going right through it down the stairs.

The air was humid and warm toward the end of the stairs and a pungent blend of chemical smells hung in the air. A cavernous room opened before him; blue-green ambient light illuminating the scene... dusty, voluminous library; a wide array of braided herbs, preserved small animals and other dubious remedies in glass keepers; laboratory glassware, stacked and sorted, draped with the cobwebbed patina of the centuries. Suspicious life forms were being kept alive in saline tanks that gurgled and steamed the air. In a prominent niche in the wall was a skull wearing a crown displayed on a burned pelt of ermine and a torn Arkenstone banner.

A raven perched behind a bookshelf took sudden flight with a loud screech frightening Damien. The pipe organ music stopped. The visor on the suit of armor standing by the wall was raised, and a pair of pale blue glowing orbs within followed his steps. At once, a dozen candles around the room alighted.

"Who dares disturb my peace?" a gravelly voice demanded.

"It is only I, Damien. I seek your services on an urgent matter."

"I know you not!" said the grizzled old man who appeared before Damien, "and I offer no services. Be gone with you." The long gnarled fingers of Draconus spill over the head of his twisted briarwood cane. He was taller than Damien by a foot and his face had recorded every line from the previous three centuries. His over-sized eyes were transparent pale blue for having lived in the unlit dungeon for such an extended period.

"I must go to Hell, if you please, sir," Damien replied.

It was probably the first time in two hundred years that Draconus had laughed. As he came to see that Damien was serious, it drew ever more hearty derisive laughter. "You may go to Hell any way you like, but now you must leave while you are still able."

Damien was crestfallen. He knew his destination lay

beyond his reach without some supernatural advocacy. Stuffing his hands into his pockets, his fingers fell upon an old good luck piece. His eyes widened.

"I have this," he said, retrieving the golden coin from his pocket. His father had found it lying in the street and gave it to the young Damien for good luck, after the liquor store clerk had refused it as not being proper currency. But then there was the time that the lady next door, who had claimed to be a Wiccan in secret, recoiled in fear at the sight of it and implored him to "lie the damned thing upon the railroad track and be done with it!" So he was pretty sure that it held some special property, good or bad. But at the time he couldn't bear to part with the only gift his father had given him.

For a moment, Draconus appeared to recognize some special quality in the talisman, but then scoffed at his paltry offering. Just the same, he pocketed the coin and led Damien to a great book lying open on the table. He turned to a page near the back in an appendix of maps.

"Here," said Draconus, tapping a map with his claw-like fingernail.

Damien studied the map and read the inscription: *Take ye the Olde Vale Road to the Forest Enchánte; there wilt ye find the Trail of Oblivion to delivereth thee to the Caverns of Avernus.*

"It is a fool's errand," said Draconus. "You will not survive it." He consulted his gazing crystal, muttering to himself.

Damien endeavored to burn the image into his mind: Trail of Oblivion... Caverns of Avernus. As his eyes wandered around the room, they came to rest on an intriguing implement: It was the Staff of Merr from the legends... *which holds great power for those who know how to use it, and great danger for those who do not.*

Draconus looked up from his crystal. "You are but a sad mortal, your story is revealed to me," he indicated the gazing crystal. "You bring me nothing of value and I am not interested in your fate."

"I beg of you," Damien implored, "can you not spare a bit of magic to help me on my journey?"

"If you would prefer to travel as a salamander," said Draconus, "I shall oblige! I do not suffer fools well. Now, be gone!"

Draconus retreated back through the doorway and Damien, dejected, shuffled toward the stairway. He knew of no other who could offer any meaningful assistance. Damien looked back over his shoulder one last time, regretting the circumstances that led him to a desperate conclusion. A moment later, he was sprinting toward the stairway with the Staff of Merr in hand.

* * *

Starting down the mountain road with the old fortress shrinking in the distance behind him, Damien was already feeling burglar's remorse. The powers of Draconus were great, but might there be some distance where one could feel safe from his wrath? How long before he realized that the Staff was missing?

Damien reached the edge of town by nightfall. He was reminded of his younger days as he nabbed a pillowcase from a backyard clothesline. On the days when his father didn't come home to feed him, he would make the rounds in the alleys. Some trash cans paid off better than others: three-day old muffins from the bakery, mostly-good apples and pears from the grocery, carrots and potatoes from the farm stand. The pillowcase filled, he waited by the railroad track, just beyond the station. When the train arrived, he climbed into a boxcar, disappearing among the crates. As the train lurched forward, he formed a bed from sacks of grain and closed his eyes. It was a long ride to where the map began, and he would need as much rest as he could take.

After an hour, the train passed through Aeneid, the next town on the line, marking the furthest he had ever strayed from home. He had gotten that far when he ran away from home on the same train years ago. It pained him to remember that day when the other kids held him down on the playground lawn and took turns pounding on him. Even that little blonde girl that sat beside him in class kicked him in the leg, mocking him over his ill-fitting and tattered clothing. His father had to collect him at school that day and beat him all the harder for it when he got home. That portly red-faced cop, Constable Virgil, had stopped the train and pulled the young lad from the boxcar. Then, on the ride home, castigated young Damien for the entire trip, admonishing him of the perils of the vagabond life, complete with grisly accounts of cases he himself had investigated.

Sleep would not come easy in the boxcar, often jarred awake by the sudden loud clanking of the steel wheels clattering across an intersection; at other times, shaken from his slumber by visions of vicious hellhounds or the angry visage of an evil conjurer.

His mind was stuck in a loop: Surely there must have been something he could have done to save Rachel in the first place from Wickersham. If only he had not invited her onto the stage to sing together, if only he had not gazed into her eyes and lost himself there. His sadness escalated, he now placed the blame on himself for her death. "I fear it was my very love for you that had poisoned you after all, my dear Rachel," he said to the empty darkness.

* * *

Damien awoke to the unsettling rocking motion of the dusty boxcar. The rhythmic clickety-clack of the steel wheels hammering every anvil of rail in perfect time had put him to sleep the night before, but it was a grating sound on his waking ears. The morning sun stenciled bright lines across his face through the crevices in the wall, causing him to squint. Slanted rays cut through the dusty air revealing a disturbing silhouette. Rubbing his eyes, he could make out the figures of two men who had been watching him sleep. Sitting on wooden crates, they were both eating apples, and Damien saw his half-emptied bag of food at their feet.

"Hey, that's mine," said Damien, getting up with a start.

The two men watched him with stoic detachment as he retrieved his bag and retreated to his corner. They continued to eat while Damien inventoried the remaining contents of his bag. There were apple cores and carrot greens around their feet, along with the wrappers from the muffins he had intended to provide more than one breakfast.

"Oh, now I won't have enough for my journey," Damien said, disgusted.

"Where ya goin'?" asked the taller of the two, taking another bite of the apple in his dirty hand. Their ill-fitted, tattered vestments and open-toed shoes distinguished them as men of the road. Damien's nostrils burned from the stench of stale urine implanted there by his close encounter.

"To Hell," Damien said, dejectedly. He selected a potato from his bag and, plucking off the green shoots, began munching on it as much to satisfy his own hunger as to make sure they didn't get that as well.

"So 're we," said the shorter of the two. Damien looked up with hope in his eyes for an instant in the momentary belief that he may have traveling companions — no matter how poor the company — until he added, "Ifn we don't change 're ways."

The taller one snorted, which was probably as close as he got to a laugh. He mentioned that his name was Luther and that his shorter counterpart went by Rebus. They had boarded the train the previous night at switch number sixty-two as it waited for the southbound passenger train to pass and were on their weekend commute to Pagan County to scavenge the fish market on the Slith River.

"You had no right to steal my food," Damien protested.

"Didn't look as though you'd bought it yerself," Rebus observed.

"Anyways, we figured you owed us," added Luther.

"Owed you?" Damien asked with an incredulous tone to his voice. "And how is that?"

"Well, when we was gettin' on," Luther continued, "Ole Charlie—he's the railroad dick in these here parts—says he was lookin' for a murderer what's on the lamb from down south. Thought he might be ridin' the rails to make his escape."

"Yeah, an' he stuck his lantern in the door an' seen you sleepin' there," added Rebus, "we told him you was with us, beins that you had the grub an' all."

Damien's eyes narrowed and he rubbed his chin, not sure what to make of their story. "So why didn't Charlie eject the two of you?" he asked.

Luther launched into a rambling yarn of how they had once pulled Charlie's bloodied form away from a gang of fellow travelers who were giving him a terrible beating and delivered him to the authorities at the next stop. Being grateful, Charlie had been allowing them passage on the grounds that they didn't plunder any contents of the boxcar. "Ya see, it's all politics," he concluded, "What goes around, comes around."

"Still," added Rebus, "he did mention a reward for the feller if we should happen to see him." They both eyed Damien without further remarks.

Damien concocted a story of how he had been working at his uncle's horse ranch out west of town and was now on his way to visit his sick aunt in the north. "She's bad off," he said, "may not make it through the winter."

"Sorry to hear that," said Rebus, as the two simultaneously removed their dusty knit caps and placed them over their hearts for a moment.

Luther pulled a deck of dog-eared playing cards from his shirt pocket and began to shuffle them. Damien declined an offer to join their game, lying back to contemplate his situation. He decided he would have to disembark before the train reached his desired station, which meant he would have to do more walking than he had expected. He would also have to avoid any contact with the locals who may be anxious to apprehend any lone travelers in the interest of collecting some recompense for his capture.

He felt unsure whether to believe that the two vagabonds had bought his tale or were waiting for an opportune moment to collect the reward for their own. He rearranged the sacks of grain beneath him to form a more comfortable bed, and in doing so, caused the Staff to become dislodged from its hiding place and clatter to the floor. As he retrieved it, two angry goblins flew at him with black, leathery bat wings flapping madly. They screamed in his face as he recoiled from their attack. He shuddered in fear looking into their empty eye sockets, sickened at the sight of their gray decomposed faces.

Damien swung the Staff at his attackers with wild abandon, causing them to scream all the louder. He wanted — needed — to cover his ears but dared not release the Staff as it became apparent that it was shielding him from their vicious onslaught. Surrounded, sharp talons clawed the air dangerously close to his face. Again he swung the Staff, feeling it strike one of the horrible creatures, which then disappeared in a cloud of putrid smoke. Bounding to his feet, he chased the remaining goblin into a corner, where he stabbed it in the chest with the head of the Staff. Watching it vaporize, he choked on the foul smelling smoke, causing him to grope his way to the far end of the boxcar in search of fresh air.

Eyes wide with fear and feeling his heart racing, he fell back onto the dusty grain sacks, perplexed by the gruesome scene that had just played out before him. Glancing about, he saw that the vagabonds had vanished.

In their place, two dead rats lie on the floor, bleeding from wounds inflicted by the Staff. It was clear then that Draconus knew where he was and meant to retrieve his precious implement by any means. Damien slid open the heavy wooden door of the boxcar and kicked the two deceased rodents out into the passing weeds.

Chapter 4

The Forest Enchánte

By mid-afternoon, Damien found himself gazing out over Elysian Meadows as the clamor of the train waned in the distance. He was just beginning to accept that Rachel would be absent from his life for all of time. He had tried to think of anything else lying there in that dark, dusty boxcar — even unpleasant memories from his past. But now the very thought of her innocent soul imprisoned in Hell would be his driving force.

Too many years had he lived in wretched poverty, looked down upon by a world to which he strove with all his being to belong, to play a meaningful part in the grand scheme; to matter.

Only now, wanted for murder, he would be tried in his absence — and dutifully convicted — in the court of public presupposition. Now, even if he could clear his name by legal means, it would not elevate his standing beyond "indigent". *Suspicious* indigent. He could not go back; he had only the road ahead.

The Old Vale Road followed a tree-lined creek that wended its way along the bottom of an ancient riverbed. Damien stayed to the ridge, following the road from above to avoid any meetings with other wayfarers. The open countryside allowed his mind to unravel the various turns of recent events. Before long, his thoughts drifted to the Staff of Merr. In it, he had the power to fulfill his fondest desires. Yet without the knowledge of how to apply it, he risked grave danger.

The old legends didn't mention how one might employ the Staff, whether special incantations were required or if resolute intent itself would suffice. Might there be a flash of lightning or a clap of thunder? He would wait until he was under the cover of the dense forest to find out.

The legends did, however, mention the Enchanted Forest — a wildwood that grew thick and thorny, a place where evolutionary processes had gone corrupt and produced hideous and terrible gremlins and ogres, denizens of the dark to prey on the innocents that may stray there: Jarpadors, the winged crocodiles; Perros Diablo, the great tusked dogs; Hellbugs, clouds of winged beetles that could pick a living cow clean to the bones in a matter of minutes. These aberrations and more highlighted any discussion that made mention of the Enchanted Forest.

One that had kept the young Damien awake on more

than one occasion was the description of Hellbreath — an ill wind that wandered the road, visible only by the plume of dust it raised. Yet some devilry within would rob a man of all blood and fluid in an instant, leaving but a hollow ashen figure to disintegrate in the wind over time. Stark images of the partially-eroded figures withering alongside the lonely road tormented his sleepless young mind.

From his perch high on the ridge, Damien could see the intersection of the Old Vale Road with the Trail of Oblivion. He looked upon the crossroad as a soldier newly recruited eyes his first battleground in the distance, with alternating bouts of apprehension and determination, and a nauseating level of distress in either case. Though a soldier is surrounded by an army with a shared purpose, Damien was quite alone in his quest. Having been left on his own for most of his life, he was used to the inattention of others. But now he was overcome with a keen awareness of the crushing loneliness of facing too great of a task alone.

Descending the ridge, he noticed that a man was fishing from the bridge that crossed the creek. As he approached the bridge his mind was racing, and he paid little heed to the fisherman. Yet something in his mind's eye nagged for attention. The brown tweed frock the man was wearing was not the sort of vestment one would wear to go fishing. Still, the man paid no mind to Damien as he passed, not until he stepped off the bridge.

"You do not want to go that way," the voice behind him said. "Sundown is approaching, and it is a dangerous route."

"It is my road nonetheless, I fear," replied Damien. As he turned to address the man, he found that he was looking down the barrel of a blunderbuss.

"I'll be having that fine trinket you have strapped across your back," he said.

Damien hesitated, but he heard the pistol cock. He removed the Staff of Merr from the sash. "It's now or never," he murmured to himself.

He thrust the Staff with violent stabbing motions at the man, but nothing happened. "Die!" he commanded. Still nothing.

He saw the flash of the pistol's discharge, a puff of blue smoke hung in the air, all as if in a slow-motion dream that he was watching from somewhere else, somewhere safe. He saw the ball of lead speeding toward him and the Staff, in perfect reflex, moving to the spot to deflect the ball away in midair.

For a moment, the two stood staring at each other in disbelief. The man set about reloading his pistol and cursing while Damien resumed thrusting the Staff at him, yelling commands at the Staff with no result. Again the man fired his pistol and again the shot ricocheted off of the Staff. A standoff. Damien backed away as the man reloaded, then turned and ran down the road. He held the Staff behind him as he ran, feeling the lead shot ping off the shaft of the Staff. Damien ran on, out of range of the pistol, leaving the baffled highwayman muttering to himself as he watched his quarry escape.

Around the curve and out of breath, Damien slowed to a walk. He kept the Staff in hand now, so close to entering the Enchanted Forest. The meadowlands gave way to marshland, noticeably absent any sounds of crickets or frogs, or other living creatures. The scent of decaying vegetation hung in the cool, moist air. A wooden bridge crossed a small creek where Damien stopped to rest for a moment, and filled his canteen from the stream. As the would-be thief had pointed out, the sun was setting, and he hoped to be well down his path before dark.

As he crossed the bridge, he heard a familiar voice. "You do not want to go that way," the gravelly voice said. "Sundown is approaching, and it is a dangerous route." Hideous pale blue eyes glared at him from the hooded form — Draconus! Just as quickly, the vision was gone, bridge, stream and all.

Damien stood in disbelief for a moment. He realized then that he was unable to trust even his own eyes.

"The water was real — I felt it." He regarded his canteen, which felt full, but upon inspection was full of sand. He watched the sand flowing out of his canteen and saw his own hopes draining away. "How can I defend against such magic?"

He continued on his way, the trail growing smaller

where it entered the forest. The great trees of the Enchanted Forest reached dizzying heights, holding a dense canopy aloft in their massive arms. Nightfall arrived early in the forest. Damien located a suitable branch on which to sleep for the night. He felt safer now, embracing the Staff as his thoughts drifted away.

It occurred to him that both the vagabonds and the highwayman had been agents of Draconus, set up to retrieve the Staff. Yet it was the power of the Staff that had repelled their advances. Perhaps it was the Staff itself that prevented Draconus from harming him, not wanting to be returned to its evil former owner.

* * *

Tiny pinpricks of morning light penetrated the dense foliage, teasing Damien's eyes open. The musty forest scent reminded him too soon of his precarious surroundings. How he would have preferred to awaken on his own lumpy mattress to a bowl of tepid gruel. Instead he would tear the mold off a stale corn muffin and eat the core, then have the better half of an overripe apple from his bag. He surmised that he could stretch his meager provisions to last another two days, but he had no way to know how long the journey would take. He would have to do what foraging he could along the way. A giant dragonfly was buzzing too close to him, so he climbed down from the tree branch and set off down the trail.

The dark hues of the dense woods were painted across the surface of the small pond, effectively camouflaging it, given away only by the few tenacious rays of light that were able to pick their way through the thick canopy of leaves. A small stream trickled from the edge of the pond where he paused to rinse and refill his canteen. He had to take a cautious sip to ascertain that it was not yet another mirage. Finding the water to be fresh, he enjoyed a good, long drink. Damien placed his possessions on a large stump, then opened his shirt in order to freshen up a bit at the pond before continuing onward. He leaned over the water about to wash his face when he heard a stirring in the brush behind him. Stealing to a hiding place behind the stump, he crouched there with Staff in hand.

The visitor was a doe with her fawn, come to partake of the watering hole. The doe approached the pond, but then turned away with a start, nudging her progeny to follow. At first, the playful fawn traced his mother's steps obediently, but then turned back and scampered to the edge of the pond for a quick drink. The doe continued walking until the splashing of the frisky youngster caused her to look back. Something was around the neck of the fawn; something marked with bands of color ... a snake. Then another ... and another ... wrapped around the legs, the head ... the entire form smothered in slithering ropes that dragged the frenzied animal into the water. The water thrashed for a few moments; the doe stomped her hooves at the edge of the pond in a frantic dance back and forth along the shore, pawing the ground and snorting. Little by little, the water boiled down to a simmer and soon, all was calm. After a moment, the doe walked away, her head hanging low.

The scene caused Damien to be ill, nearly bringing up his meager breakfast. He was, however, relieved that he did not go through with washing his face as he had planned. He knew that he must take nothing for granted in this strange new world.

The trail was vague at times, owing to the dearth of pedestrian traffic. The trees were very old and gnarled. In the periphery, Damien saw faces in the contorted trunks. The faces turned back into featureless bark whenever he would look directly at them, but the peripheral visages were vile and angry faces without exception. Endeavoring in earnest to imagine a friendly face could not bring them to smile; the sap of the ancient trees ran heavy with dark spirits.

One particularly mammoth tree sat in the line of the trail, causing travelers to circumnavigate it, stepping over the large roots. As Damien rounded the rotund trunk, he was surprised to encounter a very young girl cradled between the oversized roots. She had tousled yellow-gray hair and wore a dirty yellow overcoat. Damien gave a quick scan to the area to see if there were any others about. The girl was reciting a sing-songy rhyme about dead soldiers, holding a cream-white lily that was mostly wilted.

"Will you help me find my mother?" she asked Damien. Her eyes did not blink; her skin was pallid and sallow.

Staff held firm in trembling hand, Damien asked, "Wh-where is she?"

"She came this way, but I got lost."

"Where did you get the flower?"

"From her grave."

"Sh-she's dead?" he asked, feeling his hair tingle.

"She died in the accident," replied the girl, "and then we got separated. We were hiding in a train car and the train ran off the bridge into the water. Everyone was dead. I saw the engineer and the fireman ... and you were sleeping in the train car behind us. We were all in the water. Everyone was just dead."

"But ... I am not dead."

To this, the girl could only laugh until tears flowed from her unblinking eyes. "You are dead, Damien!" she screamed. She pulled her head off and threw it at him, knocking the Staff from his hand.

The severed head glared up at him laughing, unblinking. Trembling, he took a step in retreat, but the roots of the great tree had risen from their earthly bed and ensnared his legs, causing him to fall. He landed with great discomfort against a rough stone that was standing alone in a patch of thorny vines. Recovering from the fall, he embraced the stone to pull himself from the grip of the tree roots. His hands bled from his forceful grip on the stone, cut by a sharp feature incised into the face of it that he soon recognized as his own name and date of birth, and listing the current year as the terminus.

As Damien tried to extricate himself from the thorny vines, they began a serpentine constriction, ensnaring him further in their painful grip. All of a sudden, and with all his energy, he sprung up like a cat, coming off the ground so completely as to break the grip of the vines, shredding his coat sleeves and trouser legs in the process. He landed on his back in the middle of the path, face to face with the laughing girl's head. Quick to his feet, he had to wrest the Staff from the arms of the headless girl's body that was intent on possessing it, and was roundly kicked in both shins for his trouble.

Running at top speed down the trail, ominous laughter chased him through the trees, multiplying into myriad voices. Further along, as the voices began to wane, he slowed to a halt, waiting until his breath could catch up to him. All at once, the laughter was next to him. He turned to see a raven sitting on a branch, issuing the same evil child laughter he had heard moments before. Had he imagined the girl and the entire grisly scene?

"You are dead!" the bird screeched, and then flew off. Damien remembered the raven from the castle and decided that it was an agent of Draconus sent to spy on him. It occurred to him that it was the Staff that managed to keep those frightening apparitions at a distance — it was only when the Staff was knocked from his grip that the tree roots and thorny vines were able to imperil him.

The path narrowed as he ventured deeper into the forest. At times, he was not sure that he was on a path at all. The musty air was heavy and damp, shrouding the chirp of the scant crickets and frogs that would trill among the fetid patches of marsh between the trees. On occasion, a bird would call out with a raucous scream or a whooping cry, leaving Damien to wonder what such creatures might look like, in all hopes of not finding out.

He had always liked birds before. His father used to admonish him for throwing stale bread to the sparrows outside his window on frigid winter mornings. Skyrats, his father would call them. But through them, Damien felt connected to the world somehow. It was their song that he awoke to each morning, precisely eleven hours after they had stopped singing the previous evening, he had noted. And each morning, a singular bird would begin the dialog with the same simple lyric that would sound as much like poetry as birdsong is able, before the others would join in the daylong conversation. And at sundown, precisely thirteen hours to the minute after they had begun, the group would fall silent and the leader would offer a final poetic benediction for the day. The unfailing routine, whether it was a good day or a bad day, brought order to his world ... an order that reassured him in an uncertain world.

Now there was only disconnect, no longer an order

to it all. Unable to trust his own eyes and ears, even the simplest conventions of routine were in disarray. Yet Damien realized that since the rules had changed, he could not cling to old ways but would have to learn to adapt to his new surroundings. He possessed an intriguing defense against the darkness with the Staff, and he would have to learn quickly how to wield its power.

He removed an overripe apple from his sack and set it on the broad trunk of a fallen tree. He thought that surely he should be able to turn the apple fresh and crisp again with all the cosmic energy that the Staff had harnessed within it. But then he thought, why stop there? He could have an apple pie, steaming warm with a sprinkle of cinnamon. Then why not a whole meal? A complete indulgence! A Feast of the Harvest with all the trimmings, the likes of which he had never tasted even with his eyes! Yes, that would be it — at last he was poor no more.

Holding the Staff over the apple, he wished for such a meal, but nothing happened. Again and again he tried, but not even the apple was improved. Still holding the Staff, he closed his eyes and his mind began to wander, first to grieving for Rachel, then to the frustration of not being able to go home, then back to that delectable feast, since he was wholly famished. At once, the fine scent of savory was caressing his olfactory — bread stuffing! And fresh-baked rolls dripping with butter, and...

He opened his eyes and it was all there: The turkey, the yams, the corn on the cob, the mashed potatoes and gravy, even down to the cranberry concoction he had no intention of touching, all spread out along the log on bone china laid out on fine linen. Skeptical of the treachery of illusions, he approached with caution, poking one finger into the mashed potatoes. One taste of real potatoes, however, and he could withhold himself no more, filling his plate until it overflowed. Everything was perfect — too perfect — and he was unable to stop himself from gorging on the fine cuisine. Having seconds and thirds of most everything, he noticed that the bowls of food would keep refilling themselves, as did his wine glass. He could have stayed there forever, just eating.

Damien finally reached the point where his jaw muscles were so worn out that he could no longer chew and the wine had rendered him torpid. He sat back from the table and noticed that his belly had grown to enormous proportions. He had a great deal of trouble standing; his legs threatened to buckle under his tremendous girth. All his life too skinny, he suddenly found himself nearly too obese to walk. His eyes caught a glint in the distance that caused him to focus — a pair of eyes looking back at him, glowing in the murky darkness. Then another pair. Looking around, he was surrounded by a ring of glowing eyes, closing in.

He spied a low branch on a nearby tree and willed himself toward it, though his feet moved too slowly, as in some frustrating dream. He could make out the vague silhouettes now — wolves. The scent of the food had drawn them from their dusky lair. It required all the strength his tired drunken arms could muster to hoist his corpulent self onto the branch as the wolves closed in, nipping at his ankles. Gnashing their teeth and howling, they ran in circles just below him, at times attempting to run up the tree trunk after him. The branch strained and creaked under his great weight, and his circumference increased by the moment, threatening to break the branch and dispatch him to the lupine predators. He pulled himself up to a higher branch and posited his oversized posterior into a large fork in the trunk of the tree where he reclined, gasping for breath. The wolves tore into the food in a frenzied attack, though for them the bowls did not refill, and so before long they had cleared the table, leaving naught but the dishes and the gelatinous cranberry substance. As Damien drifted off to sleep, he was wishing he had not left the Staff lying on the ground in the care of wolves.

Chapter 5

The Feast of the Great Toad

Damien dreamed he was falling and indeed nearly tumbled out of his perch in the tree before recalling where he was. It was morning, though a cloak of darkness disguised the fact. He glanced to the ground; the wolves had gone, and with them all traces of the previous night's repast. He was thankful to see the Staff still lying there, and to see that he had trimmed back down to his normal weight. Climbing down, he tried to make some sense of the previous night.

The wolves were real, he decided — possibly still in the vicinity — a thought that caused him to press on down the trail without delay. The food must have been real to attract the wolves, he reasoned, plus the tastes, the smells; the tactile pleasures of the food were more visceral than the other illusions had been to him. Though the illusion of obesity was only temporary, it was inescapably convincing at the time.

It occurred to him that perhaps the power of the Staff was such that it illustrated to the user the consequences of having one's wishes granted. After considerable consternation, he decided that had he requested a more modest meal, it may not have summoned the wolves, or at least, he would not have grown so heavy as to be nearly caught by them. The lessons of the Staff could be sobering and so the requests needed to be planned with care.

In the distance ahead, he could see a long dark wall that divided the forest. He found it strange that someone would have built a wall across the trail, but assumed that there would be a gateway available when he reached it. As he drew near, he noticed that the wall was of a rounded shape, covered with a polished layer of diamond-shaped stones that were precision fit without the benefit of mortar. Nearer still, he could see no breech in the wall, which ran so far as to disappear into the darkness in both directions. At more than twice his height, the rounded shape and smooth finish made it quite impossible to climb unassisted. He began to survey for a small log that might be of use to mount the wall, when the wall itself moved. A shudder ran the length of the great wall and it began to slide across the path. A most terrifying realization overcame Damien — he was standing beside a colossal serpent! The very thought caused him to recoil in awe. Straining his eyes to ascertain that the creature's head was not coming back for him, he could see no other way to get around it. He had little to do then but sit by a tree and wait for the tail.

Damien considered using the Staff on the serpent, but without knowing how to use it, he knew he could be putting himself in an even more precarious position. He recalled the previous evening, wanting to remember what it was that made the Staff obey him. When he wished as passionately as he was able, nothing happened. Yet when he was musing on other matters, unconcerned, it was then that his request was granted. It seemed to him that the Staff ignored outward desires, but instead sought the inner roots of those wishes to manifest, along with the attendant consequences. He now comprehended the danger at hand: He knew he could control those things he wished for outwardly, but how could he hide his subconscious desires and avoid becoming a victim of them?

As the gigantic serpent continued its unhurried progress, the tail section tapered lower until it was small enough to leap over. Damien did so, taking great care not to touch it.

The trail descended onto a lower plateau in the ancient forest, where a fog hovered above the ground. The must of decomposing logwood permeated the air. A distinctive sweet aroma sliced through the dampness, causing him to stop short. He looked around, peering warily into the dark periphery to determine the origin of the intriguing scent. A cautious detour seemed in order, as he vowed not to stray beyond sight of the trail. Damien glanced at the head of the Staff, as if to inquire as to its readiness.

Peering through the foliage, he could see a ramshackle shelter, of sorts; an interlocking collection of logs and branches piled, as if by a storm, into a great heap, leaving a hollow within and an opening on one side. A crooked, stooped figure was stirring a pot that hung from a tripod over glowing embers. A ragged gray cover was draped over the form of an elderly person of indefinite gender, alone, at home in the heart of the heartless woods.

Still out of sight, Damien surveyed the encampment. The shelter had many antlers and pinecones decorating the façade; the surrounding trees were ornamented with spirit wheels made of bones and feathers. He recalled a childhood story about a woodwitch who would cast spells on wayward children and then eat them. He knew even then that it was a yarn spun to keep the children from wandering into the woods without a care — and it worked famously. Yet Damien did not feel disturbed by the sight so much as he was curious. The doddering figure before the kettle did not appear threatening in the least.

The scent was now more powerful, a sweet blend of herbs and flowers with a refreshing hint of spice — some intoxicating spice. Overlooking the scene, a wave of relaxation washed over him, leaving him in a gentle euphoria. He inhaled the scent deep into his lungs, feeling it calling to him, a subtle yet seductive calling. He rose and began to walk toward the encampment, somewhat aware of what he was doing, but utterly unable to prevent it. Drawn by unseen forces toward the odiferous kettle, he was floating, his internal gyroscope spinning off-kilter, making the ground very unsteady. He fell to his knees, crawling forward. He could then see the face: Leathery and crinkled with heavy cracks, as though made of wood. The bald pate had patches of moss where remnants of hair should have been, and small twigs were sprouted here and there about the head. The long crooked nose and pointed ears were weathered and worn. The woodwitch did not acknowledge his presence.

As the light of his consciousness began to dim, his thoughts turned to the Staff that now eluded his grasp — where did it go? A moment gone, and all was dark.

* * *

Damien awoke sometime later, finding himself tied to a makeshift table of heavy timbers. The pounding in his head, the hangover from some potent brew, was magnified by the fact that the table was inclined with his feet at the high end. Craning his neck, he could see a rough-hewn limestone trough below his head that was stained with countless bloodlettings. Crude butchery tools were arranged on a stone nearby. He tested the vines that restrained his wrists and ankles, but they were stout and firm. A quick survey of his surroundings discovered that the Staff of Merr had been given a place of honor among the collection of antlers and pinecones that decorated the front of the shelter.

The woodwitch was tanning the hide of an animal unknown to Damien, some sort of giant wild boar with blue skin and a great black mane about the neck. A dry, raspy voice chanted poetry in an ancient tongue. The hide was stretched between two hawthorn saplings and the woodwitch was behind it, tanning the exposed dermis with bits of the animal's brain, most of which was still sitting on a stump nearby.

The poetry ceased suddenly mid-stanza. Aware then that Damien was awake, the woodwitch approached, prodding him with a shaky oaken staff.

"Let me go!" said Damien. "You're not going to eat me!"

"I not eat you," croaked the woodwitch. "I trade meat to trolls."

"And what do the trolls give you in return? I'll give you double of whatever it is if you let me go."

"Trolls bring cave mushrooms from Avernus," the woodwitch said.

"I am going to the Caverns of Avernus," Damien pleaded, "I can bring you all you could desire."

"I no trust you," said the woodwitch.

Damien related the story of Rachel and how it had become his mission to rescue an angel from the talons of Lucifer. Surely, he must be allowed to complete his quest, he argued. However, his pleas went unheeded. He chose not to mention the Staff — the woodwitch was not aware of its power or it would not be a mere decoration amongst the antlers and shiny souvenirs taken from other travelers who had shared the misfortune of roadside butchery.

"Sad story," said the woodwitch. "Me sharp the blades — you die quick." With that, the tools were collected and taken to the creek nearby where a worn flat rock served as a whetstone to grind a fine edge on the metal implements.

The tapping of a woodpecker pierced the chilled air. Damien saw the woodpecker as it landed on the Staff and started to peck at it when it stopped dead still. The bird cocked its head to the side as if hearing a voice. A moment later, the bird flew to Damien's side, pecking at the vines wrapped around his left wrist, until they became perforated and weakened. At times, the woodpecker would miss the vines and jab him in the wrist, but Damien had to resist crying out or recoiling from the pain as he may have frightened away the bird. When Damien was finally able to snap his arm free of the vines, the bird took flight, heading directly to the creek where it commenced to peck on the forehead of the woodwitch. The irritated woodwitch thrashed about in the water in a vain attempt to roust the avian attacker. Damien took advantage of the diversion and unlashed the other wrist, then freed his ankles.

With his feet at the inclined end of the table and the tourniquet vines around his ankles, his feet were quite numb from lack of blood. As he slid off the side of the table, Damien's knees buckled like soft rubber and he fell on his surprised face. He had to pull himself up on the table and wait until the blood flowed back into his feet so he could walk. He was worried that the woodwitch might see him, but the woodpecker persisted in its dive-bombing attacks. Soon, however, the woodwitch was able to retrieve the walking stick and bat the pesky fowl out of mid-air. Aware that he had to make his move, Damien limped to the back of the shelter, wincing in pain. From there, he observed the woodwitch at the creek and could hear the rhythmic honing of metallic blades. He climbed up the backside of the shelter and over the top until, reaching the front, he could finally extricate the Staff from the branches that secured it.

Damien inched his way down the back of the shelter, keeping his eyes on the woodwitch, moving with cautious agility to avoid detection. As he felt his right foot contact solid ground, he eased his weight down onto it and turned to flee. He was surprised to behold a figure of beautiful female form caught in a seductive pose partway down a path that led away from the encampment. The sight of her blond hair cascading over her shoulders, running down her warm butterscotch skin appeared incongruous with the dank surroundings.

Damien's mouth began to open to voice his surprise,

but he stopped short to avoid summoning the woodwitch. Though her hair covered most of her face, she had a pleasant smile that disarmed Damien and drew him closer by one cautious step at a time. She draped herself strategically yet provocatively in the shaggy pelt of some large white creature. It was pulled over her shoulders in such a manner as to allow a plunging reveal down the front, filled with one fleshy bosom after another. She beckoned for Damien to follow and disappeared into the woods.

His feet began to follow before his mind could be made. He knew this was taking him away from his trail, leading him astray, yet he did not resist, as he knew he should. Something in her manner had made her seem vulnerable, even somewhat afraid, and Damien felt an inherent urging to offer his assistance. Moreover, his inner will was squelched by a burning curiosity, not to mention insurmountable lust.

Entering the woods, he caught sight of her ahead on the path. She moved ahead in graceful strides and Damien was hard-pressed to keep up. He watched her enter a small clearing and stop, so he slowed his pace as he approached. She was searching the underbrush all around and, once satisfied that there was no danger, regarded Damien. The two stood staring at each other for some time before she slipped the animal pelt off her shoulders and held it up, loosely covering herself in the front. She indicated for Damien to do the same and he obeyed without any thought, allowing the Staff to fall by the wayside in order to remove his jacket. Pulling his jacket off his shoulders and down his arms, he felt a sharp pain in his shoulders that pulled him backwards, landing him flat on his back. Sharp claws dug in to Damien's shoulders, restraining him from struggling; his hands were caught up in the jacket, effectively tied behind his back. He was surprised to see a second set of blond tresses belonging to the one holding him down.

His mind awash in hormonal opiates, he welcomed the approach of the other. Imagining the tryst that would surely ensue, he wasn't prepared when she pounced and landed straddling his abdomen. Hovering over him, her angelic lips parted to reveal multiple rows of needle-sharp teeth.

Close-up now, he could see that she was covered with a fine flesh-colored fur with facial markings that resembled mascara and lipstick. Even the supple breasts that he had admired from afar were nothing more than markings in the fur. Animal mimicry used to draw men to their deaths. Her wavy golden mane, now in disarray, revealed her previously concealed feline ears and those intense green slotted eyes. The predator had taken her prey without a fight. She sat bolt upright and, thrusting her head back, let out a long howl to summon the others in her hunting pack. Distant replies echoed through the woods and she let out a melodious yowl to signal her location, but it was cut short. Damien saw a wooden shaft protruding just above her left breast, a trickle of blood beginning to form. She eyed the arrow that impaled her with astonishment; a flesh-colored paw moved up to touch the feathers, to see if the bloodstained shaft was real.

At that same moment, the claws in his shoulders released their grip and the presence above him fell away. He looked up at his captor in time to see another arrow pierce her rib cage. Damien watched her face as disbelief became agony, then agony gave way to resignation. He thought that he had actually witnessed the soul of that beautiful but deadly predator escape its earthly host and ascend into thin air. As she fell over, he rolled out from under her. Two dead creatures lay beside him on the path, their bronze-colored and ivory-striped backs ending in short whip-like tails. He fumbled with his jacket, noticing the woodwitch standing nearby with bow in hand, preparing another arrow. He tensed his muscles, wincing, waiting for the arrow to strike him.

"Another tiger nymph comes," the woodwitch warned.

Damien righted his jacket and was on his feet in time to see another tiger nymph bounding from the under-brush. The arrow struck her in the shoulder, causing her to scream. She pulled the arrow out and, throwing it down, started straight for Damien. He lunged for the Staff, swooping it up just as she pounced. He rolled onto his back and braced himself behind the Staff. She stopped, transfixed in mid-air, remaining in a state of levitation as Damien was able to get up and walk around her. A gentle nudge sent her floating harmlessly to the ground.

"Stick is magic," observed the woodwitch, eyeing the Staff. Damien felt a tap on his shoulder. Startled, he turned suddenly, but saw nobody there. When he turned back, it was the woodwitch who held the Staff. Damien stared at his empty hand in disbelief. The woodwitch flicked a bit of orange dust at him that hung in the air. Damien was overcome by a dizzy spell and closed his eyes for a moment. Upon reopening his eyes, he found himself in the camp of the woodwitch, once again bound to the bloodletting table.

* * *

The woodwitch was busy using the Staff to transform the encampment: The ramshackle shelter was now covered in a heavy layer of thatch and even had a door; the rusty kettle was now a steaming cauldron full of wild game stew. Rising up as much as he was able, he watched the woodwitch take a large toad from its pen and place it on a stump. He heard the murmuring incantation and watched in amazement as, in an instant, the toad grew to the size of an elephant.

The giant toad let out a bone-chilling roar just before it lunged forward, devouring the woodwitch, Staff and all, in a single gulp. In desperation, Damien pulled on the restraining vines until they tore at his wrists, watching the giant toad move ever nearer. The sharp edge of the table was beginning to wear at the vines, but it was not enough. Lunging at Damien, the toad succeeded only in knocking over the table, pinning Damien underneath. Save for a stump that caught the edge of the heavy table, he would have been crushed. So heavy was the table that as it fell over, it severed the vine that had restrained his wrist, nearly taking his hand in the process. Bruised but not broken, his free hand struggled to undo the remaining restraints just in time to watch the great toad disappear into the darkened depths of the forest.

Sifting through the rustic implements within the shelter, Damien found a bow and a quiver of stone-tipped arrows that looked to have been freshly carved. A few arrows on a shelf had blackened tips, and a small bladder of black paste nearby appeared to be the source of the substance. He presumed that it was a tranquilizing agent and shoved it into his pocket. He also located a newly-whetted knife that found a place in his belt. He set off after the marauding amphibian, following the trail of destruction.

The toad had left behind a wide swath of broken saplings and trampled shrubbery in its wake that led Damien to the edge of a wide ravine. Long skid marks entrenched in the mud stretched down the steep embankment all the way to the bottom. There, the cattails and sawgrass were flattened and the path continued

Damien Goes to Hell

along the base of the embankment. Damien followed along the ridge, spotting the creature from above. He picked out a tree with branches convenient for climbing in case the toad should take exception to being wounded with an arrow. It was a short climb for the beast and his defenses were too meager. Dipping one of the arrows into the black paste, he realized that he had no idea how long the toxic concoction would require to take effect, or if it would even work at all, so he used copious amounts of the stuff.

The first arrow Damien had ever let fly found its mark in the flank. He had aimed just behind the head but a target so large and so close would have been hard to miss entirely. The giant toad let out a loud bellow but then continued to amble along the ravine floor. The next arrow ricocheted off the toad's hard-scaled back, but after several more good shots, and more raucous bellowing, the beast began to slow its pace. Little by little, as Damien followed, the toad's forward motion ground to a halt.

He climbed onto a tree limb for a better view and decided to wait a bit before going down to investigate. The memory of the woodwitch being swallowed whole was too fresh in his memory to tempt fate.

As Damien sat, he noticed a disturbing motion among the underbrush that carpeted the floor of the ravine. Something rustled through the foliage unseen, then several things at once, advanced toward the motionless toad. Before long, the foliage was teeming with life, all paths converging on the wounded beast. A short, fat creature emerged from the underbrush carrying a spear. A wide porcine face baring menacing tusks; a snub-nosed pig that walked upright. The raggedy vestments were a combination of crude homespun and leather hides. The trolls heard the bellowing behemoth and had come to investigate.

Several more came out from their cover, moving as one in a slow motion dance. The first one touched the toad with his spear; the rest of them stopped, breathless. The great toad did not move. Then, jabbing the toad in the side with his spear, the first troll signaled to the others that it was safe to advance. Soon, dozens of trolls had gathered about the unconscious beast and were speaking in their peculiar and primitive parlance.

The trolls divided into groups; some used their axes to chop down a few of the locust trees that grew on the floor of the ravine, cutting them into logs and stripping off the bark; others gathered vines and braided them to use as rope. In a short time, they had constructed a platform next to the toad by lashing together several of the small logs, and set the platform across several larger logs that would be used as rollers. They tied ropes onto two of the legs of the toad, then dozens of the pig creatures took up the lines and, pulling in unison, rolled the toad over on its back onto the platform.

A group of reinforcements had arrived from the troll village bringing lunch to the workers. As the group was on break, Damien realized that he might not be offered a better chance. His movements were very slow and deliberate — if one of the trolls was to look up, he could easily have been seen. He recalled the woodwitch having mentioned the troll's fondness for human meat. Fortunately for him, the trolls' attention was focused on the strange creature that had wandered into their realm.

Damien stole up to the hidden side of the toad and plunged his knife into its belly. He made an incision and reached his hand in to feel around, but realized that it was a futile gesture. He continued the incision, ripping along the entire side of the toad. All at once, the cut let loose and the guts came pouring out in a loud splat. In a moment, he was surrounded by angry leathery faces, threatened by spear and axe and tormented by angry voices.

Damien spotted the Staff sticking out of the reeking pile of entrails, but it was out of his reach. For a moment, he feared that he would become the appetizer course for the great toad feast in the troll village. The trolls, however, did not attack. They began to withdraw in silence, backing away from Damien with fear in their eyes. Damien failed to understand the sudden change in their demeanor until he heard a guttural growling sound above him. A sleek brown wildcat with fiery orange eyes and large saber teeth was poised on an overhanging branch, tensioned like a spring and ready to pounce.

Damien waded into the evisceration and, dove onto

the Staff. He rolled onto his back, holding up the Staff just as the wildcat leapt down at him. In midair, the saber-toothed monster shrank to the size of a house cat, landing head first in the entrails. The confused feline hastened to disappear in the underbrush. The trolls, having witnessed this sorcery, ran as fast as their short legs would carry them toward their village without a backward glance.

Damien washed up in a nearby stream and availed himself of the better parts of the lunch left behind by the trolls. He felt rather proud of himself to have been able to unleash the energy of the Staff at will and began marching around with his chest puffed out, carrying the Staff as his scepter. He knew he should be on his way, but felt tired from his ordeal and decided to have a rest. The trolls could return, but he would show them who was boss with a wave of the Staff. Lounging on a wide stump, his eyes gradually closed and he fell into slumber.

* * *

When Damien regained consciousness, he was having difficulty making sense of his surroundings. His head hurt where, apparently, someone had used force to further anesthetize him as he slept. His eyes were not focused and he was seeing many images moving about through his field of limited vision. He was leaning with his back against a tree and soon realized he was bound to the tree with rope, unable to move.

As the clouds in his vision began to clear, he took in a vast panorama of porcine pandemonium: He was tied to a tree in the center of the trolls' village as they prepared for a feast. Near the community fire pit, the giant toad lay on its back being tended to by the village butchers. Damien was grateful not be the center of attention. Absent the toad, the knife-and-cleaver coterie would be marking up his carcass instead.

The village was comprised of small round huts lining muddy lanes that were laid out in wagon-wheel fashion with the community fire pit at the hub. The roofs on the huts were formed with animal hides and, as was the custom, the animal skin directly over the doorway had the head stuffed and mounted in a proud fashion to indicate rank within the village. The bears and wolves enjoyed proximity to the fire pit where the squirrels and rabbits did not. Most huts bore deer and antelope mounts, their antlers silhouetted against the misty forest backdrop.

The huts appeared to be uncomfortably small, but the trolls had very few possessions and were creatures of the outdoor world. The homespun walls were splattered with mud. In fact, everything in the village had been very well christened with the yellowish clay of the region. A thick layer of clay spanned the entire village and the trolls were obsessive about trampling it flat to perfection; not so much as a single leaf or blade of grass dared to protrude from the featureless ground that had been compacted with such dedicated compulsion.

Only the youngest trolls had any interest whatsoever in Damien. A group of them stood before him, gawking at him like some kind of exhibit on display for their amusement. A young male poked at his thigh meat with his cloven hoof and began to lick his chops, evoking laughter and snorting from the others. It was the first time Damien had noticed that the cloven hoof also bore an opposable thumb. He thought, perhaps, that they were intelligent enough to bargain with for his freedom, except that he had nothing to put up for his end of the deal, and the language barrier seemed insurmountable.

His thoughts turned to the Staff. He was lost and would have great difficulty finding the place where he had last seen it. Then he realized that he would be able to follow the trail of destruction that the trolls had just created by hauling the toad to their village. He would have but to find where they had entered the village and follow the trail, if only he could be released from his bonds.

Damien spoke to the trolldren that were gathered around him, pleading for his release, but the young males mocked him. They tried to imitate his voice by speaking gibberish, much to the delight of the squealing young females. An elder troll happened by and admonished the trolldren for not working. He sent them away to gather more firewood for the feast. All but one obeyed, that one being the smallest female who was not a part of the clique, though she looked after them with longing in her eyes.

Damien made the whimpering sounds of a wounded puppy in hopes of establishing some level of universal communication. She looked at him and for a moment and seemed about to speak to him; instead, she just blinked her eyes and wandered off toward the blazing bonfire.

As Damien's gaze fell upon the fire, his heart sank. There, at the crest of the mountain of burning wood was the Staff of Merr. The trolls had recovered it and, being fearful of magic, sought to destroy it. Frustrated, he pulled hard against the ropes that bound his hands behind the tree, pulling harder and harder, this way and that, succeeding only in achieving acute rope-burn around both wrists. That, and arousing an army of wood ants that lived under the bark. They swarmed over his hands and arms causing the most unnerving sensation, and he was utterly unable to do anything about it. He feared that if he began to crush them between his hands that the others would begin to bite him in response. He knew he must try to relax or be driven mad attempting to resist them.

Damien closed his eyes and breathed in slow, deep breaths — something Rachel had taught him. When he sounded like he was about to explode in desperation, she would advise, "the key to your composure is in your breathing". He kept up the slow, deep breathing until he began to feel light-headed, and continued on until he no longer noticed the ropes or the ants, and he felt the whole predicament lifted from his shoulders.

He recalled the day not so long ago when he and Rachel were on that stage, their voices blended in harmony, their hearts undeniably bound. He had tried his best to save her, but he was now resigned that this would be his fate. His mental image of Rachel helped to ease his mind, though his hopes had faded. He found himself wishing that the trolls would hasten his execution and be done with it.

The sweet smell of hardwood smoke evoked his hunger and made his empty abdomen rumble and his mouth water for the food that he knew would not be forthcoming.

"Can you think of no better tortures for me?" he asked, to no one there.

A large male troll approached Damien brandishing a machete. He held the blade horizontally at about the level of his throat. As he approached, Damien winced, awaiting the impact. He did not feel the sting of cold steel, but instead smelled a savory scent under his nose. Opening his eyes, he saw that the troll was offering him a few bites of cooked meat on the end of his machete. He snatched the morsels eagerly with his teeth and found troll cooking to be of his liking. He hoped his agreeable gestures would induce the troll to bring more, but he did not return.

The meat had been spiced with rat bane and Damien became increasingly thirsty. Rat bane grew in the marshes and was known as a deadly toxin that the trolls made use of in their dart guns. In miniscule quantities, however, it added a tangy bite to food and led to a mildly hallucinogenic euphoria. Between the rat bane and the trolls fondness for fermented bog apple wine, the lot of them were soon staggering about quite carefree.

At first, Damien had attributed his altered vision to the variable color infusions of the setting sun: The bright orange highlights outlining the huts against ambient purple hues appeared surreal and grew more so with each passing minute. The illumination of the sunset soon gave way to the strobing of the dancing flames in the fire pit, which were further exaggerated by the effects of the rat bane. The faces of the trolls around the fire became flat smudges of color with crude features drawn on them.

At first he found them to be hideous, though bye and bye, he began to find their strange visages to appear quite humorous. He tried to restrain a laugh, but it would not submit to his will. He was soon laughing beyond control until he had laughed himself out of breath. Every breath he managed to inhale was forced out again as laughter until his jaw hurt and his sides ached. As hard as he tried to stop it, he realized on some level that it was his accumulated fears and frustrations boiling over inside of him that were coming out as laughter. As much as he ached from it, he felt an over-tightened spring within him beginning to unwind. It helped that the trolls had had their fill of food and wine and seemed to have little interest in adding him to the night's menu.

When he was finally able to catch his breath, a new illumination seemed to have spread over the village, though it was just his over-dilated pupils giving him enhanced night vision. The orange highlights of the flames mingled with the blue midtones cast by the full moon filtering through the trees, twisting and turning into kaleidoscopic patterns that played out across the pale ground and the sides of the huts. It hurt his eyes to look directly into the flames, though he thought he could still see the Staff among the burning embers. He was not able to tell whether he was hallucinating the bluish glow around the Staff that seemed to be providing a protective bubble or whether it was just wishful thinking on the part of his intoxicated mind.

Damien laid his head back against the tree and stared up at the stars. The heat waves from the fire caused the air to ripple and made the night sky appear as a reflection on water, the stars undulating and shifting across the inky blackness occasionally punctuated by a formation of orange sparks flying off to join them. That was the last image Damien remembered before he passed out from exhaustion.

He awoke with a start as he felt something tugging on the ropes that bound his hands, causing shooting pains against his rope-burned wrists. He was unable to see anything there because the tree was blocking his view, but he could hear something breathing, and the pulling on the ropes did not abate. In a moment, his hands fell free of the rope and swung down by his sides. He raised his hands before his face in disbelief, hearing his elbows crack from having been locked in position for so long.

He then felt the same tugging at the ropes that held his ankles and could now see the young female troll that he had seen earlier sawing the ropes as best she could using a toy hunting knife. As the rope dropped off, she scampered away in fear of being discovered. Damien knelt for a moment, rubbing his sore limbs and watching the youngster weave her way between the huts to a far edge of the village. He picked up the cut ropes. He would throw them in the fire to prevent their discovery and any subsequent investigation into who had assisted in the escape.

He looked around and noticed that all of the inhabitants of the village were fast asleep in various positions around the perimeter of the fire pit. He moved nearer the glowing remains of the bonfire, watching from behind a cart of firewood to be sure that all were asleep and that none would sound the alarm at the sight of him. For what seemed like an hour, he watched the slumbering residents shifting and turning in nocturnal bliss, sometimes tickled from within by traces of rat bane. Working up his courage, he took a branch with a hook on one end from the cart, and crept near the edge of the fire pit until he was in reach of the Staff. It did not appear to be damaged beyond being blackened by smoke residue, despite having spent the entire evening in an intense fire.

He reached out with the branch in an attempt to hook the Staff. As soon as he touched it, a wall of orange sparks shot upwards with a great deal of cracking and snapping. Damien's heart was in his throat as he peered around to see if anyone had been awakened by the sound. He wanted to wait a bit to make sure he would be safe to continue, but the heat from the glowing coals was roasting his flesh so he was forced to proceed. Each time he pulled on the Staff it would unleash a new storm of fiery sparks skyward and he would have to stop.

The flames had all died down to the smoldering embers, but his activity caused some of the wood to rekindle and new flames began to illuminate the area. Afraid of being caught, he pulled the Staff out all at once, dropping it outside of the pit. He immediately fell to the ground and rolled into a ball doing his best impersonation of a sleeping troll, in case any of them may had been awakened by the disturbance.

Damien waited for as long as his nerves would allow before reaching a cautious hand out to touch the Staff. He had expected that any material that could resist such great heat would surely retain much of it, but to his surprise and relief, the Staff was quite cool to the touch, perhaps even cooler than if it had not been in the flame. Damien had never known what material composed the Staff, but had assumed it was a lightweight wood — at least it never felt like metal or stone, though no wood was inflammable to that degree. He wondered if, perhaps, such a thing could have been fashioned from the very fabric of the cosmos itself.

As he touched the Staff, the carbon black came off on his fingers. He ran his hand the length of the shaft and applied the blacking to his face and hands, in order to more easily disappear into the night. Just before he began to creep away from the fire pit, he secured a strip of roasted toad meat as long as his arm.

*   *   *

Having spent another night reclining on a tree branch, he was up early and wanted to put some distance between himself and the troll village before they discovered his escape. Damien remembered that the trail ran parallel to the valley of the trolls, and could foresee no trouble in finding it by dead reckoning. He walked back through the woods in the direction of the trail with the Staff in a firm grip as the various events of his journey began to play out in his mind. He stopped them, determined to keep his mind on his immediate surroundings to prevent any further unpleasantries.

He pressed on though the heavy underbrush of the forest, hearing menacing sounds of unknown origins in the distance from every direction, still the trail did not reveal itself. Damien had known loneliness in his life, but he had never felt so alone as he did now. He wondered about what his life was worth, outside of answering the call of his mission. He felt a chill at the thought of wandering the forest in fruitless search, until at last some predatory monster caught him off his guard.

He happened upon a small, somewhat overgrown footpath, not age-worn enough to be the Trail of Oblivion, and it meandered off into heavy foliage in both directions. Still, he peered down the path, first one way, then the other, hoping to see a route to his advantage. He had to ultimately concede that neither route led in the right direction. He was about to move on when some glittering objects on the muddy path caught his eye. The path ran through a darkened thicket and just at the edge, a few bright yellow objects stood out against the darkness.

Wary of the omnipresent dangers, he approached with caution, more than once stopping to survey his surroundings with studious care. Convinced that he was absolutely alone, he bent to study the glimmering pebbles that lay in the path. He picked one up to examine it and, after a simple battery of tests, determined that it was, as near as he could determine, gold! Incredulous, he picked up another nougat and bit and scratched and rubbed and came to the same conclusion. The path was littered with them as if some misfortunate wayfarer had torn a hole in his sack of gold and left a trail spilling out behind him.

Eagerly, he followed the trail with golden highlights in his eyes, stuffing his pockets as he went. Damien dreamed of all the things he would have: a new house, a fine wardrobe, maybe even one of those noisy motorcars like he had seen that tried to run his old man off the road. Now he would command respect.

It was with some disappointment that he regarded the ending of the trail of gold. As he stooped to pick up the last few nougats, his eyes caught sight of the motherload — a large glistening pile of golden pebbles, half hidden in the weeds off the side of the path. He cast aside the Staff and fell to his knees, scooping up handfuls of the gilt treasure and letting it run through his fingers, eyes wide with wonder. He filled all of his pockets until they would hold no more and buttoned each with care to prevent losing any.

Startled by a noise behind him, he fell over onto his back in the weeds. He found himself looking up at a giant brown furry spider, as high as a horse and three times as wide.

Damien was frozen, looking into more eyes than he could count, watching the menacing mandibles working. The spider opened its mouth and droplets of golden dew dripped from its hideous fangs onto the ground, where they congealed into golden nougats.

Horrified, Damien tried to right himself but found he was so weighted by his treasure as to be unable to move — a clever trap that depended on the weakness of a man to ensnare himself. He glanced toward the Staff that he had so carelessly tossed out of reach.

The spider began making loud clicking noises with its mandibles. It moved forward until it was hovering over him.

"If you're going to eat me, get it over with!" Damien begged.

But the spider did not move from its guard, and continued to make the loud clicking sound. Damien did not fully comprehend his peril until he noticed, at some length away, a pack of dozens of smaller spiders scurrying up the path in his direction — the juvenile arachnids were responding to the feeding call of the mother.

With slow and steady movements, Damien unfastened the buttons of his pockets, allowing the glimmering ballast to pour out onto the ground. Little by little, pocket by pocket, he felt the weight falling away from him, watching the ravenous hoard approaching at an eager pace.

All at once, a commotion taking place nearby caught his attention. Yelping screams filled the air, and the monstrous spider was taken aback by the disturbance, turning to find the source. As the spider backed away, Damien could see a pair of two-legged pronghorns caught up in a giant spider web that crossed the path.

The two rust-colored pronghorns were struggling to free themselves from the sticky webbing, but only succeeding in getting further caught up in it. Their desperate hooves pawing the ground seemed only to excite the young spiders, already in a feeding frenzy; their sad and mournful cries told that they understood they had met their doom.

The young spiders swarmed over them and had soon

paralyzed the helpless pronghorns so as to enjoy their meal at leisure. As the giant spider was busy shepherding the smaller ones to the easy prey, Damien slid further back into the weeds. Cringing at the sight of the twitching pronghorns being devoured, he was unable to reach the Staff without attracting the attention of the ravenous arachnids.

A rhythmic pounding sounded in the distance, growing louder until a gray blur sped past him on the path. Three hungry wolves had heard the cries of the pronghorns and were intent on feeding. They scattered the spiders like bowling pins with their abrupt arrival, though the spiders were not so easily dissuaded. A great brawl ensued: The wolves crunched the spiders in their jaws like walnuts while the spiders threatened to overwhelm them by sheer number to inject them with their paralyzing venom.

With the large spider distracted, Damien crawled to the Staff and picked it up. He began backing down the path, away from the fray. As he turned to run, his path was blocked by one of the smaller spiders. He brought the Staff crashing down on it, causing it to turn into a golden puddle that quickly solidified into an impressive mound of shiny gold. Mesmerized, his eyes widened, the shimmering treasure calling to him to avail himself of riches beyond his meager dreams. His hands were drawn to it, to pick it up and embrace it, though his feet were intent on forward motion. A backwards glance revealed that the great spider had taken notice of his escape. The realization that it was his weakness for the gold that had gotten him caught in the first place forced him to abandon the notion and he fled down the path.

Part of him knew he would never have such a prime opportunity for instant wealth, but the better part of him understood that if he allowed himself once again to be wooed by greed would surely lead to his demise. Even if he could get away with it, the added burden of such a heavy piece of gold would make his difficult journey even more so.

Having walked for some time, he became concerned that he had not run across the trail. Maybe he was walking in circles — hard to know since all of the trees looked alike. In a sudden rush of wind, a raven flew past him with a loud screech and startled him. It turned and flew at his face, causing him to fall to the ground in dodging the angry bird. "Ha, ha, ha, ha," the laughter was shrill and frightening, "You're dead, Damien."

With that, the raven raced ahead, stealing something that was hanging in a tree and flying off with it. Damien wasn't able to make out what the bird had in its grasp and at first dismissed it as unimportant. Then something in his mind's eye realized that the object was a man's hat — a derby. He wasn't sure what to make of the scene, but then his eyes grew wide and he ran ahead to find the tree where the hat had been hanging. Scratched into the bark there was an arrow with the inscription "Pluribus".

Reinvigorated by his deliverance, he forged ahead with a renewed confidence. As he rejoined the trail, his footsteps were light and he was making good time. The upbeat feeling was short-lived, however. As he rounded a corner, the trail descended down a steep grade, straight down the dark throat of the Caverns of Avernus. Opaque yellow-gray sulfur fumes fouled the air. A few long-dead trees poked their twisted limbs through the toxic mist that hung over the wasteland of boiling mud surrounding the cavern entrance. The lonely wail of a coyote far away may well have been the nearest living creature. Not even buzzards patrolled these skies.

Chapter 6

The Caverns of Avernus

The inside of the cave was dry and warm, unlike the moist chill Damien had expected. Prehistoric murals on the walls warned of the many dangers that were hidden beyond. While the drawings were curiously devoid of bats, most every other type of beast or vermin was represented. There were the man-eating predators from the forest that were attracted by the warmth of the caverns in the cold season, and then there were the predators that lived in the darkness and preyed upon them. The final panel was unambiguous: A gaping open pit with human skeletons falling in headfirst.

There was a pile of spent torches along the wall, but he was able to find one with some flammable material still attached, and added bits of moss from the others. He wished he had brought more matches, as he was down to his last few, but he managed to ignite the torch on his first try. With the Staff in one hand and torch in the other, he moved ahead with cautious steps. Faces and fetishes carved into the stone to ward off evil did little to reassure him.

The trail descended to a lower level and the cave opened into a wider room where legions of skulls were displayed in small niches carved into the walls. The trappings of funerary proceedings lined the floor: Melted candles, long-empty ointment containers, half-burned parchments and riven Gospels of varied faiths. The catacombs stretched on for what seemed to be miles. The sheer number of skulls caused Damien to feel more insignificant with each new turn, knowing that his, too, would litter the earth one day. Would his skull be one displayed with some semblance of dignity on the wall? Or would it be crushed into fragments like the millions that had ended their journey broken and trampled on the floor?

As the cave began to narrow, the catacomb ended at a wide quarry-block wall, as though some had made their best attempt to conceal and contain what lay beyond for all eternity. Yet at one time, one enormous stone was forcibly ejected from within and lay shattered on the floor, leaving a substantial breach in the wall. A guard seated at the wall, clad in rusted medieval armor served as a silent sentinel as he had for many centuries. Damien thrust his torch into the opening in the wall to attempt to see inside, ignoring the inscription carved into the stone above: *Abandon all hope, ye who enter here.*

The torch burned away the cobwebs and caused the

floor to come alive with movement. He swept the floor with the flame of his torch, the Staff trembling in his white-knuckled grip as he stepped across the ill-boding threshold. Silvery-white snakes with pale pink eyes were draped over the rocks and boulders. The ceiling was illuminated by a million blue glowworms, issuing enough light to view the immense black spiders that crawled amongst them. Eyeless rats scurried between the stone formations on the cave floor, while making sure to avoid the snakes, for a meal at one of the streams of giant cockroaches that flowed from the crevasses in the walls. The spiders rappelled down onto the rats from the ceiling and bound the sightless vermin in silken cocoons to be ingested at their leisure.

Graying bones of animals and humans formed a tangled layer across the cavern floor, save for a winding path down the center. The flickering torchlight did little to hold the cave dwellers at bay, and some creatures drew unnervingly near as he passed. Crawling and slithering forms converged on the path ahead, as if hungrily awaiting his misplaced footfall. The Staff clutched tight against his chest, he moved ahead on sheer blind faith, knowing it would be otherwise impossible to traverse this path by way of even the most skilled footwork. He believed that his faith in the Staff to protect him was what instructed it to do so, yet he believed no less that giving in to fear, even for a moment, would break the spell.

The cave turned and descended in a winding spiral,

burrowing ever deeper into the stone mantle of the planet. A very dim light somewhere ahead glowed brighter with each turn; a faint humming sound, dopplering, reverberating, growing louder as he descended the dank helix. The sound was ominous and distressed; a foreboding warning, yet a hauntingly familiar siren song that beckoned him. The source of the dazzling light remained elusive, always just around the next turn. Fluctuating glowing colors, tongues of firelight in hues of azure and verdigris raced across the walls. The air grew thick and humid, laden with a pungent mix of mildew and acrid smoke.

Just ahead, Damien could make out a stone archway that led into a larger room —by the depth of the acoustics, a much larger room. Whirling light beams shone through the portal; the sound thundering off the stone walls. Entering the cavernous room, the sound reached a crescendo so loud he had to cover his ears. It took some time before his eyes could adjust to the brilliant light. From a vast hole in the center of the ceiling, a luminous waterfall flowed down into a mammoth pit in the floor. The glaring waterfall itself appeared to be the source of the aqua-tinged light, shining so bright as to prevent his direct gaze.

Waves of torrid heat rushed from the pit. He moved closer for a better view and, as his eyes began to adjust, he realized that the room offered no exit aside from the archway where he had entered. The deafening sound began to resolve itself — it was the mournful cries of the multitude of the damned, legions crying out in terror and desperation. He moved closer to the pit, keeping his eyes focused on the rim, should anything leap out of it. As he reached the edge, he could see that the gaping pit fell away to nothingness — bottomless. The waterfall dropped into the murky depths until it vanished from sight far below.

It was then that Damien realized the terrible truth: The waterfall was not falling water, but an ethereal river of condemned human spirits plunging headlong into the darkness from the world above. He averted his eyes from the sublime and surreal scene; it was more than he could bear to assimilate. But he then understood another horrible truth as well: That gaping pit was the only route to his loathsome destination.

Damien peered into the depths, at once consumed by a bitter, vacuous chill from within: He realized then that this would be the end of his life. Were he to turn away, the whole of his character would be in question for the rest of his days, and his remaining days could not number high enough to vindicate his feeble character. Having suffered the trials and tribulations of the journey and finally having reached the threshold of the point of no return, his mettle was severely tested and he was resolved not to fail himself. The many indignities and shortcomings that had comprised his meager life thus far had forged a sterling core, albeit shrouded in raggedy vestments.

Still, a weak and spiritless voice inside his head implored him to reconsider. Every living bone and ligament would pursue survival before ideology, and every muscle in his body endeavored to push him back from the brink. Yet even his daunted self realized that the road of retreat had become no less treacherous and perilous than when he had earlier plied it, and he could just as easily die there on the return trip having accomplished naught.

Even if he was to return to the only home he had ever known, he would have been tried for murder, and likely been convicted of it. And then there was Draconus, who seemed intent to retrieve the Staff at any tax on Damien's well being, should he forget his vigilance. But mostly, there would be no Rachel to sustain his heart, no oasis of color in the grayness of his dismal existence.

Nothing could go back to the way it was, even as bad as that was, it would be much worse should he attempt a retreat now. Still, it wasn't the hopelessness behind him that had been driving him along, but rather the faith in his own tenacity that had been pulling him forward.

The world outside had never afforded Damien an opportunity to prove his true worth. He had always felt that there was a giant inside of him, wanting to burst out of his timid exterior and ride high above the cheering crowds. And then there, standing at the edge of the world with great waves of heat blowing back his hair and the screams of the maligned piercing his ears, he could see with great clarity. It was never the world's place to give him a chance; it was always his to take.

The events of Damien's life careened through his tattered mind, and he grimaced as he was painfully reminded of the numerous times when his lack of confidence had deprived him of wondrous opportunity. Now the one event he had so completely blocked out as to be effectively erased from time itself ran through his mind: Damien had gotten a job as a carny at the county fair. He had shared a bottle of wine with one of the barkers behind an arcade tent and had become quite inebriated by the time the drink was depleted. At that inopportune moment, Rachel happened to be walking by and saw him sitting there. She spoke to him about how callous her father had treated her and about how she abhorred the thought of a future with Wickersham, ending with a casual offer to run away together and leave it all behind.

At first, he was dumbfounded and assumed she was joking. He couldn't imagine the beautiful rich girl giving up all to share in his mediocrity, his poverty. In his drunken state, he could only laugh. It wasn't until later that he realized the look in her eyes was hurt. He would never get the chance to apologize.

His tears were lost in the rivulets of sweat that streamed down his face. He understood then that what he did with his life, he did not do for the crowds, but for himself alone. Gripping the Staff with fierce determination, he leapt from the precipice into the abyss.

Plunging through unbearable heat, Damien wrapped his arms around the Staff in order to cover his face with his hands. Falling... on and on... like in a dream — a nightmare! If he was to die, he decided, let it be sudden, and let it be over. If he was going to survive, it was time to face the terrible foe and let his fate be decided.

With a sudden jolt, he was seized from his freefall, plucked from the air by powerful talons. Unable to move, he looked up to see the glaring eye of a griffon with great scaly wings and a sharp beak. The beast swooped low into a cavern that was lit by the glow of firelight. The cavern opened out into a vast underground chamber, where a dark green river flowed beneath in silence.

The muddy water was teeming with sinister glowing eyes peering up at Damien, so he made no attempt to wriggle free. Not that he could at any rate — the crushing talons held him so firmly that he found it difficult to fully catch his breath. The griffon flew toward a massive black stone cliff, the top of which had been carved into a towering fortress. Great spires of stone beyond the wall reflected an intense fire that raged below, out of sight. The same chorus of inhuman screams that had tortured his ears before was now emanating from within the fortress. The baying of hellhounds echoed off the high ceiling.

The griffon soared high up the cliff wall. All at once, Damien felt the great talons release and he fell free. His fall stopped short as he landed in a giant nest built on a ledge near the top of the wall. The impact of the fall dislodged the Staff and it became caught in the rough and brambled matrix of twisted vines and sticks that made up the griffon's roost. With a loud screech, the griffon awakened the two griffon cubs that were sleeping there, then leapt from the nest, swooping down along the wall in search of further prey. The siblings looked like scruffy auburn lions with the wings of bats and eagle-like beaks and claws. They attacked him without delay, nipping at his legs and arms with their sharp beaks. He struggled to extract the Staff from between the branches while trying to ward off the two ravenous attackers. When he at last controlled the Staff, the feeding frenzy ceased for a moment. There was an uneasy truce as the twins were poised for another attack, hissing and growling.

He peered over the edge of the nest and saw that it was a long way to the ground and a precarious climb down at best. Scaling the wall to the top was by far the shorter route. Step by step, he began a slow dance around the edge of the nest with the two griffons shadowing his every footstep. Reaching the back of the nest, he lifted himself up onto the rock wall with one hand, keeping the Staff in the other to repel the young griffons. Once out of their reach, he climbed to the top of the wall, swinging his leg over the cornice; the young griffons cried out for their dinner. Damien ran along the footpath that capped the top of the wall, hoping to put some distance between himself and the nest before the mother responded to the cries of her progeny.

The wall was separated from the main fortress by a deep corridor. Below, roaming packs of hellhounds patrolled the floor of the chasm. The fortress was a natural stone formation with great spires of limestone that had accumulated over many eons. He could not see beyond the wall of the main fortress, only the orange glow of intense fire from within that played across the wide stone ceiling. Just ahead of him on the wall was a guard tower from where a footbridge arched over to an opening in the fortress.

He was contemplating any alternatives to a run-in with the guards when he heard a rushing sound behind him. The griffon swooped out of the darkness with a loud screech, aiming straight for him with outstretched talons. Without delay, he sprinted with raging adrenaline to the guard tower. Sliding through the doorway of the outpost, he was relieved to find that it was not occupied, and the dust and cobwebs would suggest that it had not been for quite some time. Half a length behind, the griffon skidded to a stop just outside the doorway.

The Staff served to keep the animal at bay as Damien pondered his next move. There were three doorways in the tower: An entry from either side of the walkway on the wall, and another opened onto the bridge that led to the fortress. The griffon was busy trying them all, being rebuffed by the Staff each time. Damien could see that the griffon was determined and feared that there would be a long standoff. Rusted ancient weapons lined a wooden rack along one wall. Damien selected the least rusted halyard from the rack, however, as he lifted it, the rotted wooden handle crumbled in his hand and the large blade came crashing down, taking a chunk out of the stone floor next to his foot.

The momentary loss of focus allowed the griffon through the door. With the beast looming over him, Damien rededicated his attention to the Staff and the griffon halted its advance. The animal appeared to become bewildered for a moment, tilting its head and looking at the Staff. Damien reached behind his back and felt for a weapon, laying his hand on the pommel of a rusted sword. In one fluid movement, he withdrew the sword from the rack and thrust it into the shoulder of the beast. Although not a mortal wound, the griffon bent its head to inspect the gash, exposing its long neck to Damien. He slammed the sword down on the beast's neck with all his strength, but the blade was too corroded to penetrate. Instead, the animal became infuriated and as its head snapped up, the Staff was knocked from Damien's grasp.

Bleeding and angry, the griffon roared in Damien's face, one mighty talon suppressing the Staff against the floor. Damien roared back, swinging his sword at the head of the beast. The griffon averted the strike and parried with a great foreclaw that sent Damien rolling across the stone floor. The griffon pounced, but was slowed by its wound, and Damien again wielded the sword, putting out one of the menacing yellow eyes. The griffon reared up and let loose an agonizing howl, giving Damien the opening he needed to plunge the sword forcibly into the furry chest of the beast, dodging just in time to avoid the full impact of the powerful beak.

Winded, he fell back against the wall, watching the animal labor through its last few breaths. He eyed the few remaining weapons, should the griffon find a second wind, but none appeared to be up to the task. The great beast seemed done for, though Damien couldn't help but feel a twinge of remorse at seeing such a magnificent creature come to its end. Still, only one would leave there alive, and he was determined to be that one. At last, the griffon gave up its ghost with a gurgling sound and a final exhale.

Finally able to reclaim the Staff, Damien hurried across the narrow arching bridge to the fortress with a keen sense of vigilance, should the griffon's mate emerge from the smoky darkness. He entered the fortress, ducking into a stairwell to catch his breath. Feeling light-headed, he was breathing hard and the sulfur fumes burned his throat. He found that his canteen was filled with sand, again. Disgusted, he considered leaving it behind as it was cursed and would never again be content to contain liquid without transforming it. Then he remembered that he held the very tool to reverse black magic, if only he could learn to control it. He raised the

Staff over the canteen, entertaining thoughts of cool, clean water, but with no result. Taking a deep breath and relaxing his posture, he cleared his mind of all else, concentrating on the image of the canteen filled with water. Still nothing. He found himself trying harder to concentrate, but realized that the more he tried, the less he was able to focus. The mere act of trying, in itself, seemed to inhibit the creative energy necessary to intend the Staff to engage.

Frustrated and downhearted, he sat down on a step. He had no idea where he was, nor had he formulated any plan to achieve his mission. He did know, however, that he could not endure breathing the rancid, smoky air for long. He licked his dried, chapped lips, knowing that he was very unlikely to find any drinking water where he was. His thirst increased with his inability to do anything about it. It was then that he noticed a bit of condensation around the neck of his canteen. In an instant, the metallic surface became very cool in his hand and, as he lifted it, the contents sloshed around inside. He opened the lid and splashed some of the cool, fresh water in his hand before taking a long, deep drink.

Damien stared at the canteen, pondering what directive he had given that had caused the Staff to act. Try as he might to create an image of water in his mind, from a simple cupful to a raging waterfall, bore no results, yet to experience the sensation of thirst yielded just what was required to quench it. He saw that he had been trying to *force* creative thought into his controlled mind, and it stubbornly resisted. He then realized that creative energy must be *allowed* to enter his opened mind for it to work. That was the key — to feel rather than to think.

The unfamiliar feeling of confidence gave Damien a new outlook. His dread of the unknown began to dissipate, replaced by the courage of duty. For all I've been through, he mused, I could use a drink stronger than water. Hoisting the canteen for another drink, he was surprised by the scent of fine cognac that filled his nostrils. He took a healthy snort of it, and was preparing to take another when he recalled how he had previously failed Rachel — and himself — owing to his inebriated state. Believing that he would be much better off with no alcohol, the canteen was once again filled with water.

Having discovered an insight into the workings of the Staff, he closed his eyes in meditation, dwelling on his inability to breathe the fetid air. He took particular notice of how it hurt his throat and burned his sinuses, and how it made his eyes sting. He cleared the air with his mind first, breathing slowly, each breath more pure than the one before. Breath by breath, the air began to taste sweeter. He held a vivid scene in his imagination and gradually his olfactories recognized a familiar scent — the gentle fragrance of the park on a spring morning when the lilacs were in bloom. So convincing was the sensation that upon opening his eyes, he half expected to have been transported from his dismal surroundings. Enveloped in a pocket of filtered air, his eyes no longer stung from the smoke, even his skin felt cooled from the repressive heat.

Breathing in deep draughts of the sweet air, he contemplated his other needs. He concluded that he would need to become somehow concealed to whomever — or whatever — he should encounter. He tried his best to feel his invisibility, but seeing no difference himself, he would have to wait until he was confronted by some adversary to determine whether he would be, in fact, sufficiently masked to their awareness.

Far down the stairwell, ambient light from a distant fire illuminated the depths with an ominous blood-red glow. He did not know where he was, nor in which direction he needed to go, and considered how to request a map of some sort from the Staff. Something red scurried by on the wall next to Damien and startled him. A glowing red iguana landed on the step next to him and ran down the spiral stone staircase. He watched with bemused detachment as the crimson lizard bounded down the steps until it occurred to him that this fluorescent reptile was his Staff-appointed guide. He gathered up the canteen and Staff and trotted down the steps, trying his best to catch up.

Intense, grating inhuman wailing issued from the depths of the fortress. The further down the staircase he ran, the more the agonizing din became clear: The suffering of the damned subjected to everlasting torments and crucifixions.

Exiting the staircase through a stone archway, he entered an enormous open space. The walkway he was on was little more than a ledge around the perimeter of a vast subterranean chamber. He caught only intermittent glances of the opposite wall of the room for the thin veil of smoke rising from the lake of fire that consumed the entire lowest level; the ends of the room disappeared in the hazy distance in both directions. The center of the cavernous room was cut away, revealing many layers of floors that repeated until they disappeared into the smoke from below.

On some of the layers, Damien could make out unending lines of people who would approach the edge overlooking the lake of fire, then disgorge the large rock that they had been made to carry for some great distance through a hot claustrophobic tunnel, only to then turn back to retrieve yet another rock. He could see that the construction of Hell was an ongoing project, ever expanding to accept new inmates.

Many of the stone walls were lined with prisoners who had their heads stuck completely into the stone wall itself, deep enough to make them all appear headless. Having their entire head buried in solid stone up to their shoulders they were unable to see or hear, smell or taste, while their body remained exposed to whatever tortures and humiliations the demon squads would fancy. Thus was their retribution for failing to acknowledge pain and suffering in others, thinking only of their own well being.

Through the plumes of smoke and the deforming heat waves, Damien could pick out a few scenes in individual cells: A man watched his family being beheaded, one by one, begging for his help as he sat, paralyzed by fear. Then the scene reset itself and played out again. And again. The demons taunted the man until he cried. Again and again.

In another cell, a woman, naked and filled with desire, was surrounded by a group of men who feigned disinterest. Clearly, they were attracted, but any man who acted on the attraction received an electrical shocking that left him a whimpering pile on the floor. Men being tortured for their lustful indiscretions; a woman suffering for her unrelenting frigidity.

In a long hall on one floor, people are tied to heavy wooden tables and being eaten by animals. Many are dressed as sport hunters; some are gamblers who bet on the dogfights; still others had cruelly abused animals in an ironic display of supposed superiority.

Another cell displayed a man tied to a chair. The room was empty and the frustrated man tried in vain to escape his bounds. The greedy financier who had wanted more and more would have to do with nothing. Forever.

Gangsters and bullies who relied on their machismo were duly castrated and made to wear ballet tutus. Their aggressions removed, they were being forced to fight each other against their wills for the amusement of the demons and guards.

Cell after cell. Floor after floor.

The collective hopelessness was more than Damien could bear and he had to look away. He shuddered and felt his courage draining away. He had just peered straight into the face of the risk he had taken and it left his knees in a weakened state. Struggling to walk, he knew he must summons the strength to carry on. It was in Damien's nature to help another whenever possible, but he knew that these unfortunates were beyond his abilities and he would have to numb his senses to them if he was to avoid being enlisted in their ranks by succumbing to fear. He knew he must resist any temptation, whether compassionate or voyeuristic, if he was to accomplish his mission.

The walkway appeared to be reserved for the guards — it was deserted but for a group of them in the distance. It appeared the brutish guards had caught several miscreants trying to escape their punishing routine by hiding there, and were busy throwing them off into the lake of fire far below. Once they had dispensed of their charges, they turned and began their pounding lockstep march in Damien's direction. He retreated back into the stone archway, hearing them coming closer. Had they seen him? Or was his cloak of invisibility effective?

The guards were foul and hideous creatures, the reanimated remains of the most murderous cold-blooded warriors representing many wars throughout the history of mankind. Their bony countenances registered no emotion; the eyeless sockets penetrated even the most dense stone walls. The unison footsteps grew louder; the unmistakable stench of death invaded his filtered air as they approached. Damien peaked around the corner to catch a glimpse. One by one, the guards turned to look directly at him, causing a cold shiver to run down the back of his neck. The rhythmic footsteps did not hesitate, however. Each guard scanned the space where Damien was standing and sniffed the air, but seeing nothing, continued on. Once the squad had passed, he exhaled an audible sigh of relief. He then had to run to catch the crimson lizard, which was but a mere red dot far ahead on the walkway.

The incessant crescendo of mournful screams and cries gnawed at Damien, despite his best efforts to disregard his nefarious surroundings. His thoughts turned to Rachel; he felt as though he could feel her presence somehow, and was soothed for the moment.

Damien had seen the red lizard slip into a corridor ahead on the walkway. When he arrived, however, it was nowhere to be seen. Venturing into the darkened hall, he was without a torch, dependent on what little ambient light there was to find his way among the rubble that littered the floor. He passed by several open chambers filled with impenetrable darkness from which he felt quite sure he was being watched. In one such chamber, he thought he had seen something red move across the floor and disappear.

One tentative step at a time, he crossed the threshold and entered the room. Further in, he could see no trace of the lizard, but froze in his tracks when he heard a scuffling sound mixed with murmuring voices. And then a voice he recognized…

"Damien…"

At once the room was filled with a dim yellow glow and he could see a heavy wooden rack in the middle of the room where a feeble old man was being tortured by a pair of scaly-winged creatures with fiery eyes and menacing teeth.

"Damien, help me." It was his father. "They say I is evil and mus' pay for my sins. Tell them, son. Tell them I is a good…" His pleading words were choked off as one of the creatures turned the heavy rusted wheel on the rack, pulling his wrists and ankles in opposite directions.

"Leave him be," Damien commanded, trying his best to get the Staff to intercede.

The creatures taunted Damien, whipping the old man with leather belts. "Remember this, boy?" one of the creatures hissed. Their hideous laughter intensified as it reverberated off the chamber walls.

"Leave him be, I say!" his voice breaking as he became emotional. Frustrated at the lack of cooperation from the Staff, he tossed it aside and charged into the chamber. As he neared the scene, he stopped cold in his steps.

"Give the wheel another turn, he deserves it." It was the voice of his mother, who then appeared at the head of the rack with arms folded and an angelic smile on her lips.

"Mother?"

The rusted wheel turned harder as it reached its capacity, and amid popping joints and straining ligaments, the old man cried out in anguish.

"No," Damien cried, "Stop it! You're killing him!"

A large frame began a slow descent from the ceiling on rattling, heavy chains. In it, dozens of sharpened steel darts were mounted, set to release at the touch of the hair-trigger held by one of the creatures. "We are just beginning," it hissed at him.

"It is *you* who should be on the rack, after what you did," said his mother, whose face now became a wicked scowl.

"Wh-what do you mean,"

"You left me to die, you little imbecile!" she bellowed. "I ask you for a simple thing like chicken soup and you desert me, leaving me alone on my deathbed!"

"B-but the store was closed," he stammered, " I had to go begging door-to-door. No one would give me any..."

"You left me to die because you didn't care!"

"That's not true! I... I..."

"He *should* be on the rack, indeed." It was his old schoolmaster who now appeared beside his mother. Dressed in his foreboding black robe, he held the very ruler in his hands that he had used to humiliate the young Damien in front of the other students on frequent occasions.

'Yes, let's put Damien on the rack!" The bullies from the playground who had routinely chased him and called him vulgar names, now appeared on the periphery. "Remember when we colored your face with lipstick?" They were laughing at him.

They were *all* laughing at him now.

He crumpled to the floor crying, a broken man. "This is my life," he sobbed, "I have been living in Hell."

The chorus of laughter echoed, growing louder and louder until it became a deafening roar and Damien had to cover his ears. Brilliant illumination overtook the scene, growing ever brighter until, even with his eyes clenched shut, the glow of light still penetrated.

"Stop it, stop it, stop it," he kept repeating. He was curled in an embryonic ball on the floor, a helpless figure, when all at once, it was but his own voice he heard in the darkened, empty room. Nothing of the dreadful spectacle remained but the two scaly-winged sentries, who were busy shackling his wrists and ankles. They dragged him away, sobbing, coughing, his stomach twisted in knots.

A hidden door in the back of the chamber opened into a vast room of opulent grandeur. Golden light reflected off of every gilded surface with a dazzling effect. A lighted fountain in the center of the room spewed multi-colored liquids, giving off a strong odor of alcohol. All manner of gruesome characters milled about on the polished marble floor; some filling their glasses from the fountain, still others filling their plates from a long banquet table piled high with every imaginable type of food. A procession of culinary artists brought forth an endless assortment of regal haute cuisine to one end of the table that moved as a conveyor the length of the room. At the far end of the conveyor, an open pit in the floor received the uneaten servings to the visible horror of the starving souls chained around the edge of the pit. Former gluttons turned gaunt and emaciated, they clawed the air in a futile attempt to reach the cascade of comestibles.

A diverse gallery of onlookers occupied a row of chairs around the perimeter, smoking cigars and playing cards. The chairs were made of various animal parts that had been juxtaposed by a skilled taxidermist to form stylish furniture. Hundreds of stuffed human heads were mounted on the red-flocked wallpaper that colored the upper portions of the wall. The lower portions were filled with paintings and sculptures, all variations of the same subject: The mammoth horned beast that occupied the great bejeweled throne uplifted on a riser at the head of the room.

Lucifer.

The throne was surrounded by semi-clad reptilian females that swayed to the reverie of a string quartet of scaly-winged creatures that bowed their tormented human instruments with saw blades grating against exposed bone. The percussion section malleted their scalped prisoners' skulls with various hardwood and metal mallets in a slow syncopated rhythm while the pair of hellhounds flanking the throne howled in down-tuned harmony with the wailing and moaning of the anguished instruments.

Lucifer paid no mind to his entertainment, however. He was busy berating a guard for being lax with a prisoner by using a branding iron that was much too hot, thereby cauterizing the wounds as they were inflicted. He cut off one of the guards long pointed ears with his dull sword and made him eat it as a warning.

The hideous lizard beast on the throne wore a cape sewn together from his favorite collection of human tattoos. His gray wrinkled skin was more elephantine than reptilian and the long serpentine tail bore the markings of a diamond-back, complete with a rattle at the end. No highlights shone in his black eyes, deep-set under a sloping, heavy brow that was permanently furrowed in an angry downward arch.

Lucifer kept his enormous black wings folded behind him, unless he wanted to appear intimidating in excess, in which case the markings on the terrific span caused him to resemble a colossal cobra prepared to strike. A great golden ring hung from his snout in between a pair of yellowed tusks that jutted from his lower jaw. Firelight glinted off the gold medallions and chains draped around his wide neck; the magnificent jewels in his crown sent brilliant-hued highlights scattering across the floor whenever he moved his massive head. Two curved horns protruded from the crown, their sharpened ends glimmering crimson with fresh blood.

The guards deposited the haggard Damien at the foot of the throne.

Chapter 7

The Inner Chamber

"What is this pathetic creature at my feet?" demanded the booming voice.

"I-I am Damien," his voice cracked as he tried to steady himself. "I h-have come to strike a bargain with you."

The Beast threw back his great head and howled with laughter. "You are a fool! Why should I bargain with you when I could just have you thrown in the lake of fire for the amusement of my friends?" He made a sweeping gesture with his giant hand to indicate the motley guests who had gathered nearer to witness the impending doom of the strange visitor.

"You are a gambler, are you not?" asked Damien.

"That I am," replied Lucifer. "I am also a cheat and a liar, so you will lose in any case."

The small crowd tittered and guffawed.

"I will have to take my chances," said Damien.

"And what is it that you would bargain for, fool?" Lucifer raised his immense scaly wings nearly to the ceiling of the large chamber. His vacuous black eyes projected the coldness of death, yet the flaring nostrils glowed of an unnatural fire within. His long forked tongue darted in and out, licking his chops in anticipation.

"A friend of mine... named Rachel," began Damien, "Asmodeus, your archduke, stole her and I have come to claim her and redeem her soul."

The gallery let out a collective "Awww," and then began laughing at Damien.

"Nothing do I care of redemption!" Lucifer bellowed. "But since you have come all this way, I will prolong your inevitable fate for the amusement of my friends."

Scattered applause grows into cheering as all of the remaining occupants in the room had by then pushed their way into the semi-circle surrounding Damien.

"What is in it for me?" Lucifer asked, "

"If I lose, you keep my soul as well."

"I have no patience for your do-gooding, soul-saving nonsense," roared Lucifer. "I do not need your permission to keep your soul here — I do not need to win your little game in order to dispense with you in any ill manner I may conceive."

The creatures in the audience mocked Damien, jeering and calling out for their favorite tortures, "Let the rats at him!", "Make him fight the bear!", "Snake pit!".

"While it is true that you do not need my consent," said Damien, "the real wager is whether you are strong enough to keep your end of the deal when I win."

"You will not win!" Lucifer howled, "And if you dare impugn my strength again, I will crush you like an insect!"

Damien was hit by a blast of foul-smelling smoke issuing from Lucifer's nostrils that burned his eyes and choked him. When he opened his eyes, he was imprisoned in an iron cage, suspended high upon the wall.

"I will deal with you in good time," Lucifer said, "for now I have relevant matters to command." A select entourage followed Lucifer out of the room; the remaining crew returned to their regular debauchery, which now included throwing foodstuffs at Damien's cage.

Unable to escape, Damien fell to the floor of the cage in frustration. He had not suffered his onerous journey to become some minor trophy hung upon the wall. Without the Staff, however, he felt defenseless against the supernatural. Self-doubt sunk its venomous fangs into him, and he wondered if he might not be better off in the lake of fire. How could it end this way? He closed his eyes, sobbing, and drifted off to sleep.

* * *

Damien awoke with a start, reminded in an instant of his precarious situation by the heightened murmuring of the crowd. He saw that there was a second cage hanging next to his, and that it was occupied by the fair Rachel in a state of suspended animation. His calling to her did not rouse her, and the cage was much too far away to reach, though he tried anyway. Before he could react, his cage was shrouded in acrid yellowy smoke. Damien then found himself coughing and wheezing on the floor in front of Lucifer's throne, free of his cage.

"I have decided your fate," says Lucifer, "you will be forced to watch as my demons and assorted minions defile and brutalize your friend for all of time."

The crowd lets out a cheer, whistling and hooting in the direction of Rachel's cage. "Me first!", "After me!".

"And if I win?" asked Damien, "Then she will go free?"

"You will not win," said Lucifer. "Even if you could win, I would allow only one of you to leave. Now how much do you love her?"

This drew uproarious laughter from the crowd.

"That's not good enough!" Damien demanded. "You will take Wickersham in my stead as well."

"Why should I allow you to set the terms?" Lucifer bellowed.

"Are you the gambler you said you were?" Damien asked. "Then surely you have nothing to fear from such a mere mortal as myself."

"I am a gambler," said Lucifer, "and so I will raise the stakes as you say. I will bring Wickersham here in any case. I will make it his duty to kill you personally, since we don't suffer the living here. Then I will freeze you in a block of ice with your eyes glazed open, and you will watch for a thousand years as he ravages your beloved virginal friend. To Wickersham, she will appear decomposed and worm-ridden, her eyes rotted from the sockets. That will be his lot for killing her. But to you she will appear nubile and very much alive, begging you to save her, pleading for rescue from her torment. Pray, have you any other conditions?"

The audience taunted Damien, ridiculing his defiance.

"What shall be the contest then?" Damien asked.

Lucifer pointed one great talon towards the chamber off of the main room from whence Damien had arrived. He was told that a large granite boulder now occupied the center of the room, along with a hammer and chisel.

"I will have that stone sculpted into a graven image of myself. The likeness must be flawless, though flattering, and the final sculpture will be rendered of solid gold."

"But that is impossible," Damien protested.

"I told you that you would not win," Lucifer said.

The audience burst out in uncontrolled laughter and jeering. Lucifer gestureed to a servant who bore a velvet pillow with a small sand timer on it.

"And it must be completed before this hourglass runs out!" The miniature timepiece that the attendant placed on the table could hold no more than five minutes worth of sand.

Once again, Damien was overwhelmed by a cloud of bitter yellow smoke that choked him and burned his eyes.

As the smoke cleared, he found himself all alone in front of a huge granite boulder in the dimly lit outer chamber. He could see the silhouetted edges of the two guards posted just outside of the door. Simultaneously, they turned and looked at him, murmuring to each other and chuckling about his fate. He picked up the chisel and hammer and started to work on the huge stone. He had to stall for an agonizing minute before the attention of the sentries were no longer on him so he could slip closer to the door to be able to search the pile of stones where the Staff had fallen.

It was no small relief, then, to see part of the silvery shaft protruding from behind the rocks there. Continuing to pound on the head of the chisel with the hammer so as not to arouse the suspicion of the guards, he retrieved the Staff and hurried back to the boulder.

Damien concentrated on creating a likeness of Lucifer. All his best attempts produced nothing more or less than the original block of granite. He was aware that he was trying too hard, feeling unable to let go of the consequences of failure. All his energy was concentrated on focusing his mind rather than achieving the task at hand. He spotted the hourglass in a lighted niche in the wall — nearly halfway finished!

Then the rock began to move and change shape. In his distracted state, the likeness he created was more than true to form: It came to life and lunged at him, knocking the Staff from his grip. The vicious granite beast chased him across the room, snorting and growling, thwarting any attempt by him to retrieve the Staff.

Damien removed a torch from the wall and used it to keep the beast at bay for the moment. He tried to maneuver closer to the Staff, but the snapping stone jaws were coming dangerously close to claiming an arm or leg. He could feel Rachel's presence in the next room and realized that his coming for her had put her at great risk. He was compelled to reach the Staff, but glancing at the hourglass, determination turned to desperation.

He rushed forward at the stone beast, pushing the lighted torch into its face and hitting the body hard with his shoulder. The crushing impact hurt Damien much more than the beast, nevertheless, the beast did fall, giving Damien the moment he needed to reach the Staff. In an instant, the beast was next to him, separated only by the width of the Staff.

Searing pain gnawed at his shoulder; the hourglass ran empty. Eye to eye with the beast of stone, he heard a familiar voice speaking softly in his mind.

"Damien, you are my savior," said the disembodied voice of Rachel. "My heart was empty because I felt unloved. For that, I was living in my own hell. But you have shown me just how much love there was by the unselfish sacrifices that you made to rescue me. I could not have dared ask that of anyone. You have my eternal gratitude."

The voice faded into the dense acrid smoke that was

filling the room. In a moment of clarity, Damien knew that he had achieved what he had set out to do, to set free the heart of his beloved Rachel. In that, he was already victorious. In that timeless moment, he caught but a glimpse of a polished golden beast before him. Lucifer was there, roaring in protest, though the sound seemed distant, muffled as though he was hearing it in a dream. Through the swirling smoke, he saw Lucifer alongside his gilded likeness glaring down at him. A sudden loud blast knocked him backwards onto the cold stone floor, just before all went black.

In his mind's eye, there was etched an indelible image of Wickersham lying on a stone slab with demons piling on gold bricks until the crushing weight caused him to cry out. And there he would stay.

* * *

Damien awoke to snow falling on his face. His shoulder hurt and he had a sharp pain in his back. He was lying on the grass amongst decrepit tombstones. As he began to get his bearings, he realized that he was lying in the Wickersham graveyard. Propping himself up, he could see the coffin that Rachel was to be buried in. The lid was closed, and he stood up to further inspect it. He opened the coffin and saw that her presence had been restored. He placed his hand on her shoulder — he could finally say goodbye.

He found himself wondering if the entire episode was

but some vivid and unreal nightmare. Perhaps he had hurt his shoulder in a fall against a tombstone ...

It soon occurred to him, however, that the sharp pain he had felt in his back while lying on the ground was no longer troubling him. Curious, he walked back to the spot where he had been lying and found the Staff of Merr cradled there in his snow-frosted silhouette.

* * *

Damien visited the good Pastor Wilkins at the old stone church to see to it that Rachel received a proper interment. The pastor expressed his deep regret at the absence of her lovely voice from his choir, and was visibly pleased at the prospect of having her nearby in a well-tended site. He dispatched the groundskeepers at once to hitch the wagon and retrieve the coffin. Damien caught a ride into town on the back of the wagon.

"You should get some rest, son," the pastor called out after him, "you look like Hell."

"No, reverend," Damien assured him, "Hell looks much worse."

The snow clouds had parted and left the day clear and bright. He was very tired and wanted nothing more than to go home, but he had another stop to make first. Damien dismounted the wagon as it passed the precinct house, trudging up the steps to the office of the town constable. There, he hoped to clear his name in Rachel's murder.

"I will require a court-appointed attorney," Damien said to the constable at the desk, "as I have no money."

"On the contrary," Constable Virgil replied, "Old Man Wickersham came clean just before he died. He signed a confession in my presence stating that he had, in fact, murdered the young Miss Hart. Such was his grief, he said, that he could no longer live with the burden."

"He killed himself?" Damien asked.

"That's the odd part," Constable Virgil said, "we locked him in a cell by himself, but a moment later found naught but a burnt patch where he once was; the wooden bench burnt in half. Coroner called it spontaneous combustion — a man burns up all at once for no apparent reason."

"That's bizarre," Damien said.

"I wouldn't believe it if I hadn't seen it myself," the constable said. "But you have been exonerated and are free to go." Constable Virgil sat back in his chair eyeing Damien over the tops of his bifocals with his ever-suspicious scrutiny. "Just you keep your act clean, son."

Damien bounded down the steps a free man. He returned to his room and for the first time in his memory, felt at peace with the world. It was clear to him now that he was the master of his own destiny, and that he could make a difference.

And with the Staff at his side, he could make an even bigger difference.

Damien moved to the window, opening it a bit to

hear the singing of the sparrows. From the depths of his pockets, he produced three shiny gold pebbles. He stared at them in his hand for a long while before setting them on the desk. Then, noticing something scrawled into the dust on the corner of his desk, he could make out the lettering: "Pluribus". And just above, a crudely drawn pair of wings.